THE HAYLEY MYSTERIES

THE HAUNTED STUDIO

HAYLEY LEBLANC

Cover design by Maryn Arreguín/Sourcebooks
Internal design by Michelle Mayhall/Sourcebooks
Cover and internal illustrations by Alessia Trunfio

Published by Sourcebooks Young Readers, an imprint of Sourcebooks
P.O. Box 4410, Naperville, Illinois 60567–4410
(630) 961-3900
sourcebookskids.com

Cataloging-in-Publication data is on file with the Library of Congress.

Source of Production: Versa Press, East Peoria, Illinois, United States
Date of Production: May 2022
Run Number: 5025879

Printed and bound in the United States of America.
VP 10 9 8 7 6 5 4 3 2

In loving memory of my brother Caleb, who taught me that no matter where you are in life, if you stay true to yourself, you're already where you're meant to be.

CHAPTER ONE

I'VE NEVER BEEN SO SCARED IN MY LIFE.

But I have to press forward. Everyone else is too chicken to go inside the haunted trailer on this dark, spooky morning. What will be inside? A clue? Something that will help me solve the mystery?

I touch the silver doorknob slowly. The latch gives. The trailer door creaks open with a banshee-like wail, and dust wafts out in a huge, gray cloud. A hairy spider lurks in a web by the window. My heart pounds as I poke my head in, and...

"Hayley?"

I whip around with a yelp. My beloved cat, Salmon, who I've been holding in my arms, squirms in annoyance. Standing behind me are my two best friends, Aubrey Rivera and Cody Smith. Aubrey, who's tall, dark-haired, and thirteen—same age as me—has her jean cuffs rolled, and her soccer jersey is covered in dog hair from her giant Saint Bernard. Cody is twelve, a little taller than Aubrey, and has sparkling blue eyes, white-blond hair, and a wry prankster's smile. They're both staring at me like they don't know whether to laugh or call an ambulance.

"Are you okay?" Aubrey asks.

"And what were you saying about solving the mystery?" Cody adds.

Oops. Have I been talking out loud?

I turn around and look at the trailer. It's *my* trailer, and as far as I know, there's nothing mysterious inside. My name is Hayley, and my friends and I are actors—this is a TV set in Los Angeles, California. We star in a show

HOLLYWOOD
HAYLEY

called *Sadie Solves It.* I play Sadie, the main character, who's an amateur sleuth. Mysteries are Sadie's life—in fact, one of her catchphrases on the show is "I eat clues for breakfast." (I giggle at that when the writers aren't around. I mean... What would clues *taste* like? Donuts? Bacon?)

Aubrey and Cody are Sadie's on-screen friends, Kiki and Markus. The three of us solve a mystery an episode. Today is the start of our second season—which is a *huge* deal. If your show goes to a second season, it means people like to watch you. For me, that means even more time to spend with my best friends.

But this morning, I also feel a little...nervous.

"I was trying to get into Sadie's character," I tell my buddies, adjusting Salmon in my arms. His fur is silky black, and he has glowing yellow eyes—the perfect Halloween cat. "It's been a while, and I feel rusty."

Our show has been on a break for three months. This is our first official day back at work. Aubrey, Cody, and I reunited yesterday in our special tree house in my backyard, and today, we get down to business.

Cody reaches out to stroke Salmon under his chin. "So you're sneaking around, looking for something to investigate?" He holds up his hands. "Not judging. I love that for you. But you nearly gave me a heart attack!"

"I just want to be the best Sadie I can be," I insist.

Cody loops an arm around my shoulder. "You already *are*."

"Aw!" Cody always says the nicest things. "C'mon, group hug!"

The three of us squeeze each other tight. I suspect we're all feeling nervous. It's not just because we're starting a new season either—we're also at a whole new studio. Last year, we shot *Sadie Solves It* on a soundstage way out in the Valley, a part of Los Angeles that's to the northeast of the city, full of studios, but pretty remote.

However, because the show was so popular, the network moved us to Stage Five at Silver Screen Studios this year, right in the center of Hollywood! You know the streets with the stars on the sidewalks? *That's* Hollywood. My trailer has a perfect view of the famous Hollywood sign on the hill!

But it's a big change for all of us. It kind of feels like how it was when I went from elementary to middle school—all-new buildings, all-new people, a whole new schedule. Our old set in the Valley felt like a comfortable old Converse sneaker, worn in all the right ways. I knew which table in the old studio's commissary—that's a fancy word for the cafeteria—had the wiggly leg. I was used to the smell of the cedar trees near my old trailer. We even had a resident dog, Popcorn, who belonged to a producer on a show one stage over.

But this place? When my parents dropped me off at Silver Screen this morning, everything felt just a little bit... off. There's no comfortable hum of traffic from the freeway like there was at the old studio. I hear they don't have a frozen yogurt machine in the commissary. There's no

Popcorn the dog! Some of the faces are familiar, brought over from our old team, but a lot of people are strangers.

Also, it seems like everyone takes things a little more seriously at Silver Screen. It's barely 7 a.m., and crew and staff are already rushing around, headsets on, clipboards in hand. I spot Tina, who worked at craft services at our old place, carrying a crate of goodies. Craft services are the amazing people who bring the actors meals and snacks on the set. I give Tina a wave, grateful for someone familiar. She turns and waves back.

"Hayley Bo-Bailey! Made those banana muffins you love—and got some tuna for Salmon!" Tina gestures at the palm trees that jut over the buildings. "Isn't it amazing to be in Hollywood now?"

"You know it!" I answer back.

It's true: despite all of this being new, I do *love* Hollywood. There's something so historic about this part of town. Practically in front of every building is a plaque saying that some important film star once lived there. I love walking past Grauman's Chinese Theatre, where they've held the Oscars, and imagining myself sweeping up the red carpet to win an award someday. Getting the part in *Sadie Solves It* has been my proudest achievement, so it feels fitting that I get to shoot the show actually *in Hollywood*.

"*There* you are," calls a voice.

The three of us turn. Cody groans inwardly. Coming toward us is ten-year-old Amelia Hart, who plays Pepper, Sadie's little sister. Her brown pigtails stick out from the sides of her head like two paintbrushes. Her gray eyes dart back and forth. Amelia is a drama queen, a major snoop, and she has bat-like hearing. I swear, she can hear gossip two miles away in the middle of a thunderstorm.

"How long have you guys been here?" Amelia looks us up and down, moving slightly away when she notices Salmon. She claims she's allergic, but secretly, I think she's just afraid of black cats. "Do you have your scripts yet? What's the episode about? Pepper better have good lines this year, or I swear I'm quitting. Why haven't I gotten mine?"

"Hello to you too, Amelia," I mutter. "And no, we don't have our scripts. No one got theirs before you." Amelia is *constantly* worried she's being left out.

As if on cue, Paul Chin, the show's creator, steps onto the little landing outside Stage Five, where we're shooting the show. He spies us and smiles. "How are my stars? Want to come on set? I'd love to introduce you to some people."

He gestures to a guy who's stepped onto the landing behind him. To our surprise, it's Morton York, a producer who created this other kids' show called *Motor Clowns* that was using Stage Five before us. It had been unexpectedly canceled mid-season, which was why we were able to move in. Honestly, I can't believe the show ever made it on air—it was about race car–driving clowns. Personally, I couldn't get through a single episode without feeling a little weirded out by all that clown makeup. Guess I wasn't the only one.

But even though that one show was a flop, Morton's

famous—he's won a ton of Kids' Choice Awards, has a million followers on social media, blah blah blah. My friends and I exchange a glance.

"What's *he* doing here?" I whisper.

"Didn't you hear?" Amelia has her know-it-all voice. "Mr. York's consulting on season two of *Sadie Solves It*." She stands a little taller. "I've been talking to him a lot. He's looking to cast people in a new movie, and I think I have a great shot. Last one there's a rotten egg!" She sprints for the door to Stage Five.

Aubrey rolls her eyes. We're all on the same page when it comes to Amelia's annoyingness.

We walk over to the stage as well. As I head up the ramp, I notice a plaque on the wall bearing the names of all the other shows that have filmed here. A lot of the names are ones I recognize. There are even some really famous movies, and the dates go all the way back to the 1960s. I feel an excited shiver. Soon, our show's name will be on the plaque too!

I push through the heavy door that leads to sets. The stage is freezing. All stages are. That's because the lights on the sets get really hot, and that makes the actors sweaty, but sweaty people don't look so great on TV. The crew makes it extra-chilly to balance things out.

Workers are rushing around, building sets and arranging lighting. A few sound people rush by. There's a crash in the distance, and someone laughs. I stare up at the rafters. The soundstage is at least three stories high.

"Hayley?" Aubrey pulls on my sleeve.

When I look up, the three of us are standing in a corridor, but Paul and Amelia have vanished. The huge building has become strangely quiet, suddenly—all of the banging and hammering has stopped. The only sound is Salmon's motor-like purrs. Maybe the workers took a coffee break all at the same time?

"Paul?" I call out. "Amelia?"

My voice echoes. No answer.

I feel a surprising gush of warm air. It's like a blast

you might feel if you're on the sidewalk and a big truck whooshes by. But there's no truck, obviously. No *nothing.*

"Wha...?" I whirl around. My heart skips a beat. "What's going on?"

"Did you feel that?" Aubrey whispers.

Next, a light on the wall near Aubrey flickers. And then, a light near Cody clicks off, bathing us in darkness.

"Who's there?" Cody exclaims.

But in the very next moment, the air turns frigid again. The lights snap back on. Even the hammers start back up at a regular rhythm.

"What just happened?" I whisper. Everyone looks freaked out.

Then I hear a new voice.

"Don't panic," someone says, "but I think you've just met the stage's ghost."

CHAPTER TWO

When we turn, we see a scruffy guy in his early twenties. He wears a plaid work shirt and ripped jeans, and he holds a hammer in one hand and a walkie-talkie in another. I don't recognize him from our old studio in the Valley.

"I-I'm sorry," I stammer. "*What* did you just say?"

"I'm Mike." He offers his hand for us to shake. "I build your sets. Worked at Silver for a few years now. You didn't hear? Thought I already told you kids—it must have been another group."

"Hear what?" I ask impatiently.

Mike smiles mysteriously. "Classic Hollywood story. Some people think this place is haunted."

"Silver Screen Studios?" I cry. "Are you serious?" I feel nervous. Part of me wants to call Mom and Dad and tell them to come get me.

But Aubrey jiggles excitedly. "You're kidding!"

Cody waves his hand and scoffs. "There's no such thing as ghosts."

"There might be in Hollywood." I look at my friend. "Remember that open-air bus tour we took last year? All the ghost stories they talked about?"

"Yeah, the piano player at that comedy club on Sunset Boulevard," Aubrey adds. "The people would hear music even when *no one was sitting at the piano.*"

"And Fritz?" I remind Cody. "At Grauman's Chinese Theatre?" The tour guide told us that the famous theater has a resident ghost who'd worked at the theater years before and never left. Everyone there knows Fritz. They aren't even afraid of him.

I look at Mike. "So who's haunting this place? Do you know their name? Do they try to be in the scenes? What do they want?" My mom often says that when I get excited, I ask so many questions and don't give the other person an opportunity to answer. But I just want as many facts as possible. I want to understand.

Mike chuckles. "I'll try to answer as much as I can. Gather round."

He gestures to a small couch near the craft services tables, and we sit. Well, Aubrey, Salmon, and I sit. Cody leans against the couch with a frown like he thinks all of this is nonsense. I also spy Paul down the hall. I remember that he wanted to speak to us, but now he's deep in conversation with Monique, our show's director.

Mike rubs his hands together. "First of all, Silver Screen Studios was founded about eighty years ago, during the golden age of movies. Back then, many of the films were big, spectacular productions—musical numbers, dancing, great costumes, the works."

"I love musicals," Aubrey gushes.

I give her an encouraging grin. Aubrey is a beautiful singer, but for whatever reason, she's afraid to sing in front of other people. Her secret, deep-down goal is to be on Broadway someday, or maybe cut a record.

Mike nods. "Long ago, Silver Screen Studios was filming a big musical. There were two teen starlets, Betty and Ella, competing for the same lead role. The director couldn't figure out which girl he wanted to cast, so he had both of them come to the first days of shooting, figuring he'd decide then."

Cody makes a face. "That must have been rough."

I agree. Casting is the toughest part of being an actor. That's when you go to "try out" for a part. The competition is fierce. There are so many talented people competing for the same spot.

"It was day one of rehearsals," Mike says in a low, spooky voice. "Betty and Ella were dancing their hearts out on this huge spiral staircase on the set. The director said he was going to decide which girl got the part after this particular dance number, so it was important they both did their best. Their feet were flying. The dance had them climbing to the top of the stairs. The music got louder and louder. Both the girls wanted to prove *they* deserved the role. But then..."

He takes a deep breath and looks around at us. We're all on the edge of our seats.

"Then *what*?" Aubrey cries.

"Betty fell off the top step," Mike says sadly. "It was a long drop. And... She didn't make it."

We all gasp. "That's terrible!"

Mike nods. "There were rumors that Ella pushed her. She didn't want Betty to get the part." He shrugs. "But that was never proven."

"So Betty's the ghost?" I'm aghast with a mix of excitement and horror.

"Well, if you choose to believe in ghosts," Mike says. "Some say Betty's never left Stage Five. Rumor has it that

she doesn't want anyone to succeed—or any show." He gives us a knowing look. "I mean, why do you think *Motor Clowns* was canceled so quickly?"

Because the show was about clowns? I almost say.

"Anyway, that's the story," Mike says, standing and grabbing his walkie-talkie. "Is it real? Who knows? But that's Hollywood for you! All kinds of weird stuff happens in this town." At that, he walks off, whistling.

My friends and I stare at each other in shock. I have to say, I've definitely experienced a lot of *firsts* today.

First time on a soundstage in Hollywood.

First time meeting a new crew.

And the first time maybe meeting someone else too.

A ghost.

CHAPTER THREE

After Mike heads off, I realize what I need to do. I grab my friends' arms. "Group meeting. *Now*."

"What about Paul?" Aubrey whispers. "He wanted to talk to us."

"Paul can wait." This is big. *Really* big. Besides, Paul is still talking to Monique. He's using expressive hand gestures, which means they're having a disagreement. This might take a while. I just hope Paul doesn't have a run-in with Betty the ghost too.

That is, if Betty is even *real*.

We head down the ramp, across the alleyway, and into my trailer. It's a basic movie-set trailer with a couch, a table, a mini fridge, and a bathroom. Someone has sprayed it with woody vanilla, my favorite scent. I can finally put Salmon down, and my kitty gratefully stretches his legs and then hops up on the windowsill.

But then, a shadow fills the doorway. It's Morton York, the famous producer who's helping out with season two. He catches the door before it can fully close.

"Hayley, right? And...Cody? Aubrey?" His gaze flits between us. "Everything okay? I saw you run out of there like the place was on fire."

I can feel my friends shift. Does Mr. York know about Betty? Did she haunt *Motor Clowns* too? Should we ask him?

But maybe he'll think we're being silly. We all want to impress this guy—it's really true that he can turn actors just starting out into major stars. How amazing would it be if he cast all three of us in his new movie?

"We're great," I tell him, smiling broadly. "Just getting ready for the day."

"And really excited you're here, Mr. York," Aubrey adds.

"Call me Morty." His eyes crinkle as he smiles. "Okay, I'll leave you to it." He steps down from the trailer's door. "See you soon!"

After he's gone, I shut the door and face my friends. "Okay. *What* do we think?"

Aubrey looks at me strangely. "What do you mean? This is incredible! I've always wanted to meet a ghost! Haven't you?"

"Not really..." I mutter, nervously twisting the

sapphire ring I always wear. Sapphire's my birthstone, and Sadie's. Last season, Sadie wore a sapphire necklace, but the necklace kept getting caught on things during my scenes. At the end of the season, the writers decided that Sadie lost the necklace in one of the final cliff-hanger moments. Sadie's mom gives her the new ring as a replacement at the very end of the episode. Sapphires give Sadie the strength and courage to solve mysteries—and me too.

I'm not surprised Aubrey wants to meet a ghost. She's always up for adventure. Aubrey's one of those people who's calm in the scariest of situations—like in the final moments of a major soccer tournament, or when she has to give a speech in front of a group of kids, or even when she has to get a filling at the dentist. In fact, the only thing that scares her is singing in front of people. Cody and I are the only people who've heard her great voice.

"You don't want to meet a ghost because you don't *believe* in ghosts, right, Hayley?" Cody asks. "There's no scientific proof that ghosts exist." Cody might have a wicked sense of humor, but he's practical and doesn't like taking risks...*or* believing in things like ghosts.

"I don't know if I believe or not." I look at Aubrey again. "You honestly think Betty is real?" It feels strange to call a ghost by her name.

"Totally!" Aubrey's eyes shine. "Think about it. Betty's probably trapped in Stage Five, bitter about her tragic death. What if we could help her? Maybe we could set her free! Let her live her best ghost life!"

Cody sighs in exasperation. "Aubrey, that is the silliest thing you've ever said."

"What?" Aubrey's hands fly to her hips. "Why?"

"Because you can't talk with something that doesn't exist."

"But what about that *whoosh* we felt?" I ask him. "Those flickering lights?"

He shrugs. "Lights flicker. And the whoosh was probably just the air vent."

"What about the rumor that Betty doesn't want

anyone to succeed? What if she wants that for our show? What if she's trying to scare us away?"

"Nothing's going to scare *me* away," Cody says stubbornly, crossing his arms. "Not even a ghost."

"I know." I nod. Cody has worked so hard to get here. While Aubrey and I live in Los Angeles year-round, Cody, his two moms—Jada and Chris—and his little foster brother, Teddy, have a home base in Texas. While we're shooting, Cody and Jada rent a little apartment in LA, while Teddy and Chris stay in Texas.

But that's hard on everyone. Cody misses his family. The goal is to get everyone in one place, preferably California, but Cody's moms don't want to relocate the family unless Cody's acting career is secure. *Sadie Solves It* getting a second season is a big step toward convincing the whole family to move, but they haven't quite decided yet.

"Also," Cody goes on, "there have been lots of TV shows filmed at Silver Studios. Why have we never heard about a ghost before?"

"Maybe they've kept it a secret," Aubrey argues. "No one would want to shoot here if that rumor got out."

"What about Mike making it sound like Betty was the reason *Motor Clowns* shut down?" I add.

Cody rolls his eyes. "*Motor Clowns* was canceled because it was a bad show!" Then he looks guiltily out the trailer's little window and says, quietly, "Sorry, Mr. York."

We all think for a moment. Then Cody shrugs. "Guys, that ghost sighting was nothing. I'm sure of it."

"You're probably right," I agree, shooting an apologetic look at Aubrey. "We probably shouldn't get too worked up about this."

"Party poopers." Aubrey raises a finger. "But if it happens again? Promise me we'll do some investigating."

"Okay," I say nervously. My heart starts to pick up speed. I'm secretly kind of afraid of ghost hunting.

"I know it sounds scary," Aubrey says, as if reading my mind. "We'll have to be brave. Just like Kiki says on the show: *The first rule of solving mysteries is don't be afraid!*"

Aubrey's character, Kiki, is fearless. She's always the one chasing down the bad guys.

"*And* we'll search for the logical reasons," Cody adds. "Just like what Markus says on the show: *There's always an explanation.*" Cody's character, Markus, is the brain of the group, a math and computer genius who has an encyclopedic knowledge of names, faces, and trivia—a lot like Cody in real life. Markus is always the one who breaks down how a crime could have happened according to physics and science.

And Sadie? She's the leader—and I'm kind of the leader in real life too. My friends look to me to make the final call.

"Good point, both of you," I decide. "We'll keep our eyes and ears open. Just like Sadie, we'll have to *eat clues for breakfast*!" I snicker, and everyone else does too.

Whatever this ghost thing is, it's definitely a mystery. It looks like my friends and I not only play sleuths in TV but also will become sleuths in real life.

CHAPTER FOUR

The three of us don't have much time to think about ghosts for the rest of the morning, though. Paul finds us and hands over our scripts, and soon enough we're in hair and makeup and trying on outfits in the wardrobe department. After a quick table read—which is where all the actors read through their parts of the script, start to finish—it's time to rehearse and film.

Often, in TV shows, scenes are filmed out of order. It has to do with the budget and what makes most sense with what actors are on set which particular day. Although this

Sadie Solves It episode starts with Sadie in her town's library, where it's been reported that an ancient book full of magical pizza recipes has been stolen from the rare books room, the first scene today is one much later in the mystery. In the scene we're shooting today, Sadie and her little sister, Pepper, are at Giovanni's Pizza Shop, trying to track down who could have stolen the spooky book of recipes and what they might want with it. Footprints shaped like chef's clogs have led Sadie and Pepper to Giovanni's. It makes sense that a pizza maker would want the ancient book, since the recipes are rumored to enchant someone into craving pizza 24–7.

Right now, I'm crouched down, shining a flashlight under a dining table with a checkerboard tablecloth. Amelia, as Pepper, stands behind me, waiting to see if I've found anything. Sadie and Pepper are working on this mystery together. Amelia really fought for that with the writers—she complained that Sadie's little sister wasn't in the show enough, and that Sadie and Pepper should team up. The writers went for it.

"The book's not here," I recite. It's my first line.

Amelia—as Pepper—slaps her sides. "But how can that *be,* Sadie? The footsteps led us straight to this place!"

"Sometimes, the clues don't lead where we want them to go," I say. I stand back up. But suddenly, I feel warm air on my back.

I freeze. Is it the ghost again? *Betty?*

I tilt my head, waiting. No lights flicker. I don't feel the warm air again. Maybe it was nothing?

I look at Amelia, continuing my lines. "It's all about trying to figure out if someone would have motive, Pepper. And Giovanni—"

"Cut!" Paul calls, before I can say the rest. I stop and look up.

Paul comes over from behind the camera and looks at me, puzzled. "Everything's really good, Hayley. Really. But you seemed a little...distracted. What was with that pause in your lines? That's not how we rehearsed it."

"Sorry," I say, biting my lip. Had my pause been that obvious?

Paul pats my arm. "Don't worry. It's the first day, new studio, blah blah blah. Let's try it again, okay? Just remember—Sadie is also really wise about solving mysteries. And she wants to teach her little sister about how it all works." Then he glances at Amelia. "I like your eagerness, Amelia. Very Amateur Sleuth."

Amelia does a fist pump. "You hear that, Mom?" she yells over the set wall.

"I heard, baby!" calls a voice. "You're amazing, as always! Mr. York thinks so too! Don't you, Mr. York?"

I try not to groan. Amelia's mother, Mrs. Hart, is sitting in Video Village, watching our every move. Video Village is this little setup of screens and directors' chairs where writers, producers, and sometimes even network executives watch the scene as it's being shot.

While most people's parents, including my own, come every few days to make sure things are going well—we have chaperones who look after us during the day and tutors who help us with schoolwork—Mrs. Hart plops herself down at

Video Village every single day. She always hogs the front seat right by the TV monitors too, her tall, fluffy hair blocking everyone else's view. And she always calls out praise to Amelia, sometimes even while the camera is rolling. I guess in Amelia's case, her annoyingness is genetic.

I also can't help thinking about how Morton York is sitting in Video Village too, perhaps right next to Amelia's mom. Does *he* think Amelia's acting is good? Better than mine? Was Amelia telling the truth when she said she'd been talking to Mr. York a lot about his new movie?

"Hayley? We ready to go again?" Paul calls.

I jump. *Whoa.* I *am* distracted. I need to get my head back in this scene. It's just first-day jitters. Only... *Did* I feel a whoosh just now? And Betty, the ghost—is she real, or not?

Don't think about her.

I roll back my shoulders. "Yep. All good."

"Great." Paul looks at Jasper, the cameraman, who luckily I've known from the very first day of shooting season one. "Rolling."

I shut my eyes, channeling Sadie. I remember when I tried out for the role. I'd been so nervous, I'd picked off all the pink nail polish on my thumb. But as soon as I'd gotten into that audition room and said Sadie's first lines, all the worry melted away. I *was* Sadie, through and through: curious, determined, and not the type of person who gives up. *Or* gets distracted.

Yes. Now I can feel myself plugging into Sadie's character. When I open my eyes again, I'm ready.

I crouch down, shining the flashlight into a crawl space where we think the spooky book of spells might be hiding. I can sense Amelia behind me, and, suddenly, I believe she really is my little sister Pepper, not annoying Amelia Hart. I also truly believe that she and I have followed the clues of the missing book all the way to the pizza shop, and the only thing that matters is returning the book to the rare book room in the library, where it belongs.

"The book's not here," I sigh, really feeling the disappointment.

"But how can that *be*?" Amelia says in her typical drama-queen way. "We followed all the clues!"

"Sometimes, the clues don't lead where we want them to go. It's all about trying to figure out if someone would have motive." This time, the line feels good. Genuine, like I'm saying it from my heart. "And Giovanni? Why would *he* want a book of spells? His pizza is already amazing. He doesn't need some magic words to make it better. I think there's more to this than meets the eye."

Nailed it, I think. Paul's going to love that performance.

But when I wait for Amelia's next line, it doesn't come. I move from my crouch position to check on her. As my flashlight hits Amelia's face, I see that she seems to be in a trance. She stares toward the ceiling, her eyes wide.

"Psst," I whisper. *"Amelia?"*

"I..." Amelia's eyelids flutter. All of a sudden, she crumples to the floor.

"Darling?"

That's Amelia's mother. I can hear her director's chair

scrape back, and her high heels click on the wood floor as she heads out of Video Village. "My honeypie! Are you okay? Did you faint again?"

I cross my arms, wanting to groan. Last season, Amelia was famous for "fainting" when she forgot her lines. Of *course* that would be the time just when I got my lines absolutely perfect.

I glance over my shoulder at Aubrey and Cody, who've come to check out what's happening. Cody gives me a look of sympathy.

"Baby!" Amelia's mother crouches down at her daughter's side. She pulls out a little spray bottle and starts misting Amelia's cheeks. "Come back to me, my star!"

The water does the trick. Amelia's eyes pop open, and she draws in a big breath. Everyone steps back to give her some air. Mrs. Hart helps Amelia to sit up, smoothing her hair back from her face and tut-tutting over her like she's just come back from the dead. The droplets of water have smudged the cakey foundation our makeup artist, Vee, uses on all of us to make us more camera-ready.

"What happened?" Paul asks in a concerned voice. "Do you feel sick?"

"No," Amelia whispers. "I-I don't think so."

"Then why did you pass out?" Cody sounds bored. "Forget your lines again?"

"Not at all." Amelia suddenly looks frightened. "I saw something. Up there." She points at the rafters with a trembling finger. All I see are wood beams crisscrossing the ceiling. "It was...*terrifying*."

"What was it, sweetheart?" Mrs. Hart asks, clutching her daughter's hands. "Tell me, please!"

Amelia lets out a whimper. Suddenly, I know what she's going to say even before she says it. "I-I think it was...*a ghost.*"

CHAPTER FIVE

"WHAT SHOULD WE ORDER?" I STARE AT A LIST OF MENUS ON my iPad. "Chinese? Burgers? Tacos?"

"No tacos!" Aubrey declares, making a face.

"Right, right." I've forgotten Aubrey hates tacos. "Can we agree on pizza, then?"

"Only if we can get it with pineapple," Cody says.

"Grossest topping ever," Aubrey mumbles.

"You can pick it off," Cody tells her, and Aubrey throws a pillow at his head. The pillow misses, sailing straight out the tree house window and onto my lawn.

Salmon, who's prowling around the property, pads over to the pillow and sniffs it.

We're in my backyard tree house, our safe space. Dad built it for me when I was nine, saying it was so I could have some privacy. The thing is, my house is plenty private already. I don't have any brothers or sisters. All I have to do is close my bedroom door. So for a long time, I didn't use the tree house much. But then Aubrey and Cody came along, and everything changed.

We first started coming up here shortly after becoming friends, using the tree house to practice lines and gossip about the set. We also play marathon sessions of *Minecraft* (my favorite video game) or *Call of Duty* (Aubrey's). Even the delivery services know that when we place an order, they're to deliver it to the tree house, not my family's front door.

"I'm ordering." I tap the screen and finalize the pizza takeout. Then, I flop back on a pillow that didn't fly out the window. "I need food, after this day," I say.

"Same," Aubrey and Cody grumble.

We fall into troubled silence. Amelia's ghost sighting delayed filming on *Sadie Solves It* for a while. First, security climbed up to the rafters to make sure nothing was up there. By the time we got the all clear, Paul had learned the "rumors" about Betty, and he sat us all down and explained that sure, Hollywood has lots of ghost stories, but they're all just myths.

"It's not real," Paul urged. "There's no ghost."

I'd noticed Morton York standing behind him, listening. But Mr. York didn't say anything to back Paul up. Maybe that was because he thought otherwise. Maybe it was because Betty the ghost ruined his show, and he was scared she was back.

Or maybe it was because he thought it was ridiculous.

Cody sighs heavily. "*I* didn't see a face up there, did you?" Aubrey and I shake our heads. "It was probably just a reflection. Or maybe something random floating up there, like a plastic bag. Remember when the dove got caught in our old soundstage? It could have been something like that."

"And it *is* weird we haven't heard about these ghost stories before," I agree. "You'd think a ghost at Silver Screen Studios would make headlines."

Then, I have an idea. I grab my iPad and type in *Silver Screen Studios Ghost* into a search engine, just to make sure I didn't miss something.

Results pop up quickly. I scan the options. "Okay, there's a site called *Haunted LA* that has a list of all the ghost sightings around Hollywood."

My friends crowd around as I click the link. Aubrey points out an article about Silver Screen Studios, and I select it. "This is from 1967," I say, and read, "*Several actors on a popular TV show shot at Silver Screen Studios report seeing an unknown man walking around the soundstage. When asked what the figure wanted, he vanished.*"

"A man?" Cody frowns. "I thought Betty was a girl."

"Is that the only report?" Aubrey asks.

I click back to the main *Haunted LA* page. "There's a little mention of Silver Studios here, but just as a 'potential ghost hot spot.' No more details. Nothing about Betty." I tap the keyboard some more. "In fact, I don't see any stories about a starlet named Betty falling off a staircase on Stage Five." I try a few more searches for tragedies on movie sets. Nothing.

"See? There's no proof the story's even real," Cody says.

"Maybe, maybe not," I say. "There are a lot of spooky things that happen on sets that producers keep quiet. They don't want there to be negative press about the movie. It happens all the time."

Suddenly, Aubrey hops up and hurries to a chest of drawers my dad hauled up here for all of my art supplies. Inside the bottom drawer are a bunch of board games. She pulls out a spirit board and rattles the box. "Maybe we can talk to Betty this way."

"No thanks." Cody crosses his arms. "Those things are fake."

"C'mon." Aubrey removes the lid, pulls out the spirit board, and places it on the steamer trunk that serves as a coffee table. Then, she places the glass-topped planchette device in the middle of the board, touches it with the tips of her fingers, and closes her eyes.

"Oh, spirits," she says in a spooky voice. *"We're trying to reach Betty, the dancer who tragically died at Silver Screen Studios sixty years ago. Are you there, Betty? Can you hear us?"*

The planchette jerks to the left. My heart jumps. *Is someone there?*

We watch as the planchette slowly drifts toward *Yes.* Then, Cody leaps forward and grabs Aubrey's fingers away. "You're making it move."

"No, I'm not!" Aubrey cries. "I'm communicating with her!"

"Aubrey, put it away." Cody's voice wobbles. "Please?"

We go still. Cody is usually so levelheaded. It takes a

lot for him to get worked up about something, but when he does, it's usually important.

"Okay, okay." Aubrey packs up the board and replaces the lid. "Sorry."

I clear my throat. "Why don't you want her to do the board, Cody?"

Cody looks away. "I, um, have some good news and bad news." He shifts his weight. "The good news is... Well, my moms are really considering moving here. Full-time."

Aubrey and I gasp. "To LA? For real?" I cry. "That's amazing!"

Cody holds up his finger. "I also said there's bad news. They'll only do it if things keep going well on the show. They don't want to be here if I'm just running around, out on auditions. So if *Sadie Solves It* gets shut down like *Motor Clowns*..." He takes a big breath. "Then they want me back in Texas. Permanently."

"What?" I jump to my feet. "How could they do that?"

"My moms say that once I graduate from high school,

I can come back to LA. Pursue acting again. But they miss me. They want us to be together as a family."

"High school graduation is years away!" Aubrey exclaims. Then she looks down at the spirit board box. "I get it. You don't want to talk to Betty, because you don't want Betty to be real. Right?"

Cody shrugs. "I want it all to go away." He keeps his head down, trying to hide his almost-tears—which he totally doesn't have to do around us. "This show... It's the best thing that's ever happened to me. And you guys are the best friends I've ever had."

"Same here," I agree. Aubrey nods too.

I think about our very first day of shooting, when we all met. I'd been so nervous that I wouldn't like my costars. But then, Aubrey walked in wearing one of those ridiculous hats that have two soda cans on either side and two looping straws that lead straight into her mouth. I started laughing. Cody came in next. He took one look at the soda-can hat and pulled out a pack of Mentos from his pocket. He asked us if any of us had ever done the Mentos-cola trick.

In minutes, we were behind the soundstage, launching one of the soda cans from the hat like a rocket over the wall of the studio. Later, Aubrey invited us to a sleepover at her loud, messy, chaotic house that very night. We dressed up her giant dog, binged Netflix shows, and came up with a bunch of goofy inside jokes. We've been tight ever since.

Aubrey puts the spirit board away. "Forget the séance. Seriously."

I grab Cody's hand and squeeze it hard. "We won't let you leave. We're a team—on-screen and off. Remember?"

Cody slowly nods. "Yeah."

"Good," I say. And at that moment, there's a knock on the tree house door, and I smell a tantalizing aroma of cheese, dough, sauce, and pineapple.

Pizza saves the day. *Again.*

CHAPTER SIX

But the ghost doesn't leave us alone for long.

The very next morning, as I'm eating a fruit and yogurt bowl in my trailer and studying my lines, I hear a scream. I drop the bowl and fly out to the pavement just as the door to Stage Five flies open. Amelia rushes out, her face the color of chalk.

"Get me out, get me *out*," she cries as she rushes past me.

I catch her arm. "What is it? What's wrong?"

She looks at me with terror in her eyes. "I-I saw it again. While I was rehearsing."

"What?" I ask—though I think I already know the answer.

"This...*face*," Amelia whispers. "It was a *girl*. She was looking at me like...like she was angry!" She throws her trembling arms around me. "Oh Hayley, I'm so scared! She was *floating*!"

Stage Five's door opens again, and Amelia's mother hurries out, followed by Aubrey, Cody, and a few of the other actors.

"Oh, my poor baby," Mrs. Hart coos, rushing to Amelia's side. She looks accusingly at Paul, who's run over from the offices, where the writers' room is. "Paul, why would you move us to a studio that's haunted?"

"I-It's not!" Paul cries. "I don't know what's going on!" He looks at Amelia. "Amelia, I'm sure there was no *ghost*." He says this last word very quietly. "Can you come back and do the scene, please?"

"No way," Amelia whispers, throwing a hand over her eyes. "Not if her spirit is still there."

"Come on, Amelia," Cody urges. "I was looking in the same spot you were, and I didn't see anything. Certainly not a floating girl or whatever."

Amelia suddenly looks annoyed. "Are you saying you don't believe me?"

Cody shrugs. "Well..."

Amelia puffs up her chest. "It's probably because I'm an Aquarius. I'm much more in tune with the spiritual world than a Scorpio like you."

Groan. Amelia has decided that she is the astrology expert. Anytime someone behaves a certain way, she says, "Oh, that's because you're an Aries," or "Oh, your Gemini ways are showing." And naturally, she thinks *her* sign, Aquarius, is the best.

"Kids?" Now Monique, the director, pokes her head out the stage door. She looks impatient. "Can we get back in there? We need to move on to the next scene."

Amelia crosses her arms. "I'm not going until *she* leaves."

"Who?" Monique asks.

"The ghost!"

Behind us, a small crowd has formed. There are people from wardrobe, techs, and extras, who are mostly kids. Everyone is staring, and a few people start to whisper. *A ghost?* I hear. *Is this place haunted?*

"Hayley?" A little girl who's an extra in one of the pizza scenes tugs at my sleeve. She can't be more than six or seven, and her brown eyes are wide. "Is there really a ghost? I'm afraid of ghosts."

"Me too," another kid says. "I want to go home."

"Me *three,*" says Gerald, who plays Giovanni the pizza maker—and he's an adult!

Everyone's looking at me. And I realize—it's because I'm Sadie, the lead. Which makes me the leader. I need to guide this group.

I turn to the little girl with the big brown eyes. "Don't worry," I say softly. "There's no ghost. Everything's fine."

Then I pivot to Amelia. She's now lying down across

the seat of a Silver Screen Studios golf cart like she's about to faint—*again*. Her mother fans her with a magazine.

"Can we talk for a second, Amelia?" I say in the sweetest voice I can muster.

I grab my friends, and we step toward Amelia. A few extras are still milling around, but I give them a confident, I've-got-this-all-under-control smile. Even Mrs. Hart gives

us some space. I sit down on the golf cart and pat Amelia's shoulder.

"Look, we need the show to run smoothly," I whisper to Amelia. "It's only our second day, and we're already behind schedule. Monique is mad! And I'm sure Paul isn't happy either."

Amelia pulls her knees to her chest. She's still so pale. "We shouldn't have moved to this studio. The other one was better!"

"I know. I miss the old studio too. There's nothing we can do about that now. So I think maybe you should try to not say much about ghosts, maybe?" I try to say this in the nicest way possible. "You're one of the bigger kids on this show. So you need to be a role model, you know?" *That* will persuade her, I think. Amelia always likes to be thought of as one of the older kids. She likes to have power.

Amelia frowns. "But I really *did* see the ghost. What if it happens again?"

Aubrey clears her throat. "Here's the thing about

ghosts, Amelia. It takes a lot of energy for them to make contact. So if you think you saw a ghost, you probably won't see her again. She's probably exhausted!"

Amelia tilts her head. "Really? Is that true?"

"Totally. I've read a lot on ghosts. I know all about how they work."

I almost ask Aubrey if this is true too. But then, I notice that my best friend has her fingers crossed behind her back. *Uh-oh*. Aubrey has a habit of telling little white lies to either make people feel better, protect them, or—in this case—protect our show.

But lying to Amelia might be dangerous. Like a true Aquarius, Amelia is all about things being fair and truthful. I bet she'd be furious if she found out we were just telling her things to keep her quiet.

And yet, Amelia nods like this makes total sense. "If you say so." She rises and heads back to Stage Five. As she passes the curious crowd of actors, extras, and staff, she gives them all a smile. "All good, people! Let's get back to work."

My shoulders slump with relief. "We're safe," I say to my friends. "For now."

But how long will it last? And what's up with this ghost, anyway?

CHAPTER SEVEN

Usually, hair and makeup is my favorite time. I get to sit in a big comfy chair and zone out for a while. Peter, the hairstylist, gives great scalp massages. And Vee, the makeup artist, rubs a cleanser on my face that smells like birthday cake but somehow makes my skin glow.

But today, I feel like there are bees buzzing under my skin. I can't stop thinking about Betty the ghost.

"You're scrunching your nose, honey," Vee says as she brushes my cheeks with an oversized brush. "Are you practicing being the Easter Bunny, or is something on your mind?"

I open one eye. Vee has laughing eyes and a pile of light hair on her head. As she flits around me with her wands and brushes, she reminds me of a mama bird. Her desk is littered with eyeshadow palettes, creams, mascaras, trays of fake eyelashes, and concealers in every skin shade you can imagine. I don't know how she keeps track of it all, but she says clutter is how she works best.

I slump my shoulders. "If you want to know the truth, I'm kind of panicking."

She drops her makeup brush and walks around to face me. "Wanna talk about it?"

I don't know what I'd do if Vee hadn't come along with us in the move from the Valley to Silver Studios. She's kind of like a mom, a friend, and a guidance counselor all rolled in one.

"I'm guessing you've heard the rumors?" I twist my ring around and around my finger. "About the ghost?"

Vee purses her lips. "I've heard a little something."

"Do you think she's real?"

"What? No way." She waves her hand. "I don't believe in that stuff. And for the record, I don't believe in Bigfoot, aliens, or the Loch Ness Monster either."

I sigh with relief. "So you don't feel scared? You don't want to quit?" I keep thinking about the crowd that had gathered after Amelia's second sighting. How those kids said they wanted to go home.

Vee laughs. "It's going to take way more than drama

queen Amelia saying she saw a face in the rafters to get *me* to quit. I love *Sadie Solves It.* I'm here for the long haul."

"Okay, good," I sigh. I start to feel better. It's good to know that not everyone is taking the rumors seriously.

But as I sit back, the lights in the little room blink on and off. I grip the sides of the chair. "W-What was that?"

Vee looks around. The lights are still flickering. The light bulb buzzes like it's an angry bee caught in a trap.

"I'm sure it's nothing," Vee says.

She walks over to the switch on the wall and flicks it off. Except... The room doesn't go dark. The bulb keeps flickering, almost like an invisible hand is turning the switch on and off, on and off.

"Vee?" My heart starts to pound. "I'm scared."

"It's okay, it's okay." But Vee doesn't sound so calm either.

She turns the lights on, and then off again. To my relief, this time, the light actually turns off.

Only, the darkness is scary too. I can feel my heart

thumping in my ears. I imagine a spirit drifting around the blackened room, reaching out for me, touching the side of my cheek...

I shriek. Vee flicks the lights on again, and the bulb burns brightly. I look around. No ghost. No spooky fingers, reaching out. But my heart is pounding. My face is sweaty.

Vee rushes over. "Hayley. It's okay. It wasn't anything. You've gotten yourself all worked up."

"But..." I point to the light bulb. "Why did it flicker even when you turn the light off?"

"It's an old building. I lived in an apartment in Hollywood when I first moved to LA, and the same thing would happen. Finally, I got my landlord to fix it. He said the wiring hadn't been updated since the 1950s! It's very possible that's what's happening here."

"Y-You think?" I ask.

"Honey." Vee holds my hands. "*Yes*. You're scared because someone put the ghost idea into your head. So now, you're seeing what you want to see. That's all."

I breathe out. She's right. If I'd never heard of a ghost, I probably would have thought the flickering lights were just a weird electrical problem.

"Thanks, Vee," I tell her, feeling a lot calmer.

I settle back into my chair. The lights don't flicker anymore. I have no sensations that a ghost is about to poke me in the cheek. There is something I'm worried about, though. If *I'd* gotten that scared just because of some flickering lights, it means other people might too. And then the rumor will build and build until everyone thinks there's a ghost, and people might start leaving the show.

I think about something Vee said too. *You're scared because someone put the idea in your head. You're seeing what you want to see.* It gives me an idea.

Is it possible that a person is making those lights flicker? That someone is pretending to be a ghost...and putting the ideas in our heads? But who would do that? And *why*?

I know what I have to do.

I need to solve this mystery.

CHAPTER EIGHT

THANKFULLY, THE REST OF THE DAY PROCEEDS SMOOTHLY. We shoot the very first scene of the show, where Aubrey, Cody, and I rush to the library and speak to the head librarian, who reports the book stolen. We shoot another scene where we ask cranky Mrs. Archer, the librarian on duty the day of the theft, if she has security footage from the rare books room, where the ancient book of recipes was stored, but she says that the footage was damaged.

We shoot a scene where I question Giovanni the pizza maker about why, exactly, his pizza is so tasty—is it because he's been using magic spells from the book all along? Giovanni swears up and down that he's never seen the book in his life. That scene is a good one. I get to eat lots of pizza.

By the time the afternoon rolls around, I feel better. The show is proceeding. No one seems on edge. But I haven't stopped thinking about my new theory. That someone is making us think there's a ghost.

But *why*?

During lunch break, I ask Austin, one of the production assistants, to take me for a spin around the back lot in one of the studio's golf carts.

The back lot is the part of the movie lot where we shoot all our outdoor scenes. It has a maze of streets containing any sort of building you can imagine: regular houses, city brownstones, cafés, shops, churches, schools, courthouses, and more. Most of the time, the interiors of these structures aren't decorated. Sometimes, they aren't even split into rooms. That's because usually only the outside of

the shot matters, not the inside. That's what the sets in our soundstage are for.

Aubrey and Cody join me on the golf cart, eating from take-out containers they bought from the commissary. We squeeze on the back seat and leave Austin alone at the front, like he's our Uber driver.

"Off we go!" Austin cries, hitting the gas with a jolt. He glances back at me. "Mind if I put my headphones on, Hay? I'm on the last episode of this amazing true-crime podcast, and I'm dying to know the end." He winks. "No pun intended!"

"Of course!" Actually, this is perfect. I wanted to talk to my friends on this ride. Now I can do so in private without Austin asking questions.

We start off toward the back lot, first passing a maze of soundstages, and then the Silver Screen Studios gift shop, which offers coffee mugs, T-shirts, and other stuff bearing the logos of famous shows that are shot here. As we round toward some of the residential streets, I tell my friends my new theory.

"You really think someone's just *pretending* there's a ghost?" Aubrey makes a face. "That's not nice. A lot of the younger kids are scared."

"That's why we need to figure out who it is," I say.

"Where do we start?" Cody crunches a carrot stick.

"Well, we need to find a motive," I say. "It's like in the episode we're shooting—where we have to figure out why someone wants to steal a book of magic spells."

"Right," Cody says. "Too bad we haven't seen the whole script yet. Maybe that could help us solve the answer with our ghost."

"I know," I say.

On *Sadie Solves It,* the writers and producers often only give us only our lines for the day's scenes, not the entire episode's script. They say that not knowing what comes next helps us have a "fresh" approach to our acting and reactions, so that we're discovering the truth along with Sadie and her friends. At the moment, all I know about *Sadie Solves It,* season two, episode one, is that a magic book of spells has been stolen...and that two pizza makers, Giovanni and Sal, didn't take it.

But we don't know who *did*.

Austin steers the golf cart down a street that's made to look like New York City, a mix of apartments and cool cafés. There's even a sign and entrance for the New York City subway. After we ogle them for a moment, I pull out a pen and notepad from my bag. *Reasons someone would want to fake a ghost,* I write. Sadie takes notes in the show too. It helps to have a list of suspects all in one place.

I look around at my friends. "Any thoughts?"

Aubrey chews on her thumbnail. "Maybe someone is bored?"

"Boredom." I write that down. I think of Mike, the guy who first told us about the ghost. "Mike's worked here for a long time. Maybe he wants to have some fun?"

Aubrey nods. "Mike seemed to know everything about the soundstage. I'm sure he'd be able to rig a reflection on the ceiling."

"But Mike's not here today," Cody points out. "I heard Tracey say he's out sick. And you saw the lights flicker only a few hours ago, right Hayley?"

I twist my mouth, thinking about my creepy encounter with Vee. "Okay. I'm sure there are other people who can make lights flicker." Only...*who?*

"Next stop, Small Town USA," Austin announces.

He steers us onto a street full of quaint houses, picket fences, and an adorable schoolhouse. I dwell on them for a moment, wondering which we might use for *Sadie Solves It* scenes. The building on the corner would make a perfect library.

Then I look at my friends. "Let's think of this another way. What are the weird things that have happened so far? Maybe we can figure out who was on set during each one, and narrow it down that way."

"Okay, there was the whoosh we felt the first day," Aubrey says. "You, me, and Cody. Amelia was close by. So were Paul, Monique, and Mike."

"Second time was when Amelia fainted during my scene." I'm still bitter. "I was in the soundstage, along with Jasper, Paul, Amelia's mom, and a bunch of other people." I glance up front at Austin. Even *he* was there.

"And the third is when Amelia saw the face and ran screaming from the stage," Cody pipes up. "I was in there, along with Monique and Vee."

"Was Paul there?" I ask.

Aubrey looks aghast. "Paul wouldn't do this!"

"I know, I know." I feel guilty. I don't want to blame Paul. "I'm just trying to find a pattern."

"Actually, he wasn't," Cody says. "He ran over from the offices, remember?"

"Right." I breathe out. "*Good.*" It would have been terrible if the creator of our show had been pretending to be a ghost.

Then, Cody gets a strange look on his face. "But that's smart thinking. Because there *is* a common person in all these ghost sightings. *Amelia.*"

We all fall silent. Cody shifts awkwardly. "Anyone know where Amelia was this morning when Hayley saw the lights flicker?"

Aubrey's eyes go wide. "Oh my gosh. That was around nine, right?" I nod. "I was at craft services, grabbing breakfast. And... I *saw* her."

"What was she doing?" I ask.

Aubrey glances at Austin, our driver, but he doesn't appear to be listening. We've passed Small Town USA now, and we're heading toward some more suburban streets with bigger houses.

"Amelia was slipping into a back room," Aubrey whispers. "She came out pretty quickly, making a big deal out of how she *thought* it was the way to the bathroom, and that she's so confused by this new stage's setup. But... I've seen a lot of the tech guys go back there. I think it leads to a room with a lot of controls. The heating, pipes...maybe even a fuse box."

I draw in a breath. A fuse box controls the electrical

switches in a building. Including the switch in the room where Vee was doing my makeup. Amelia could have been the one making the lights flicker.

My friends and I all look at each other in surprise. And then I say what we're all thinking. "*Is Amelia our ghost*?"

CHAPTER NINE

The conversation has suddenly become too dangerous to be held around anyone besides us. We ask Austin to drop us off in a little wooded area behind Small Town America. We claim it's because we want to bird-watch.

"Are you sure?" Austin looks nervously at the trees. "Everyone at Silver Screen Studios calls this place 'the Woods.' They've filmed horror movies here."

I climb out of the golf cart and head toward the trees. "We'll be okay."

"And I've heard there are some really great, um, *birds*

in the Woods," Aubrey fumbles. I can tell she can't think of the name of a single bird we might want to be watching.

Austin looks at us suspiciously. "Fine, but if you're not back at Stage Five by the end of lunch break, I'm coming for you."

Just to make sure no one will hear us, we head deep into the Woods. I have to admit, it *is* kind of spooky. The leaves make such a thick canopy, I can't see the blue sky. I keep hearing things scuttling under the leaves too—bugs? Snakes? Something scarier? And I nearly trip over a huge tree root and go sprawling forward, catching myself on a tree trunk.

When I open my eyes, an eyeball is staring at me. I lurch back and scream.

"It's okay!" Cody rushes forward. "It's just a prop, see?" He taps on the eyeball with his nail. It's made of plastic like something from a Halloween shop. "Must have been left over from one of those horror movies they shot here."

"Ugh, a movie about trees with eyes?" I shudder.

We find a bunch of tree stumps and settle down. The woods go quiet. We almost can't hear the traffic noises from the freeway from here. I get a chill.

Then Aubrey lets out a breath. "Could it really be true? *Amelia* is doing this?"

"We all know how dramatic she is," I point out. "And we all know how much she loves to get attention. Maybe she knew about the ghost before we did. Maybe Mike told her. And she thought she'd give everyone a good scare."

"*And* put herself in the middle of the ghost story so she can get all the sympathy," Aubrey grumbles. "But doesn't Amelia realize this might put *Sadie Solves It* in trouble?"

"Maybe she doesn't care. She's always hinting about how much she wants Mr. York to make her into a movie star," Cody reminds us. "What if she wants out of *Sadie Solves It* to do movies?"

I think this over. *Could* that be it? "So...what? She's faking a ghost to get us shut down?"

"Or maybe so she can show Mr. York her acting skills. Or maybe just to have some fun." Aubrey leans against a tree. "Let's face it, Amelia isn't the star of *Sadie Solves It.* We already know it bothers her—she made that huge deal of making Pepper more of a character. She wants to be in the spotlight in a bigger way."

Cody tilts his head, considering it. "So what do we do? Confront her? Make her tell the truth?"

"But we already tried—after she was spooked,

remember? Around all those extras?" I spin my ring around my finger worriedly. "It didn't really work."

"Please," Aubrey says. "Amelia isn't going to confess, especially with her mom always around. I think we need to catch her in the act."

"Like while she's pretending to be the ghost?" Cody asks.

"Totally! We'll have to keep an eye on her. See if she sneaks off anywhere when she thinks no one's looking. We'll have to be careful, though—she can't suspect what we're up to. If she does, there won't be any ghost sightings, that's for sure."

"Well, it's worth a shot," I say, rising from the tree stump and heading out of the Woods. "We'll split up Amelia Watch. Hopefully, we'll be able to catch her in action by the end of the day."

"And the ghost mystery will be solved," Aubrey adds.

"And things will go back to normal!" Cody cries.

"Exactly," I say.

Normal sounds perfect.

CHAPTER TEN

Operation Catch Amelia in the Act begins as soon as we get back to Stage Five. First order of business: scoring some walkie-talkies. Luckily, there are always a few lying around the set—the PAs and other staff use them to communicate, get actors from place to place, and make sure everything's going according to schedule. We turn them to Channel Three—the channel everyone else on set *isn't* talking on—and get down to business.

"Big Chicken to Rooster? Big Chicken to Rooster?" Aubrey's voice crackles on the line.

I burst out laughing. "Who?" I say into my walkie-talkie.

"It's our code names! I'm Big Chicken, since I love chickens. Cody is Rooster because he rules the roost."

"And me?"

"You're Mama Hen! Because, you know, you're the leader."

Cody's voice comes on now. "Can we just start following Amelia instead of talking about our chicken names?"

"Right," Aubrey says. "Okay. You see her, Hayley?"

I look around. I'm positioned at one corner of Stage Five, where Amelia last saw the ghost reflected on the ceiling. Aubrey is on the other side of the stage, near Video Village and some of the dressing rooms—where we felt the *whoosh*. Cody is in hair and makeup right now, so he's tied up, but he'll help out with moral support.

"Okay, I've got eyes on Amelia," I whisper. "She just finished her scene."

Amelia has just walked off a bedroom set. Monique

yells that the scene has wrapped—which is "finished" in TV speak. Usually, after Amelia is done with a scene, she checks in with her mother. But today, she heads instead for the craft services table.

Huh. *That's* not normal.

"I think she's going for a snack!" I whisper into the walkie talkie. "Or...wait a minute...maybe not?"

I watch as Amelia walks right past craft services, not even noticing the delicious spread of banana muffins that Tina made. She heads down a hall like she's on a mission. Just before she disappears into the darkness, she peers over her shoulder, like she's trying to see if someone's following her.

My heart starts to thump. This feels like something.

"Aubrey! I need backup!" I whisper.

"Where are you?" Aubrey whispers. "What's going on?"

"Amelia's heading into a hall behind craft services. It seems...*suspicious*."

"What?" Cody sounds disappointed. "I want to help!"

Then I hear Vee say through the walkie-talkie, *"Cody, I need to even out your skin tone! Sit still!"*

When I look up again, Amelia is gone. Oh no! I take a few steps down the hall, barely able to see where I'm going. I haven't been to this corner of the new soundstage yet. I notice a few closed doors. With shaking fingers, I push one open. It creaks noisily. Inside, it's nearly pitch black. Shadows shift. Is Amelia in there? Pretending to be a ghost?

"Hayley."

"Eep!" I jump and whirl around. Aubrey stands behind me, hands on her hips. "Don't *do* that!"

"Sorry." She points down the hall. "There's a staircase. She's heading up."

I can just make out the shape of someone climbing the stairs. I nod, and we climb up too, trying to be as quiet as possible. The stairs lead us to an upstairs landing and hallway. There are several rooms with closed doors. Amelia is gone again.

"Maybe one of these upstairs rooms is where she hides all of her ghost props?" I whisper.

Then Aubrey clutches my arm. A door down the hall quietly shuts. Amelia's got to be in there.

We rush down the hall and carefully twist the door's knob. The door creaks open, and we peer inside. The room is dim. A single bulb burns in the corner. It's filled with props, all right, but they're props from *Sadie Solves It*'s first season. The monster head from the episode where the whole town thought there was a creature in the lagoon. Sadie's witch costume from a Halloween episode.

"Ooh, I remember this," Aubrey whispers, pointing down at a jewelry box. Inside had been a clue that led to a secret prince. "That episode was so much fun."

"And here's those masks we wore for that creepy masquerade," I whisper, sad that they're stored all the way up here. They should be on display somewhere.

Clang. A noise at the back makes us freeze. Amelia? Is she trying to find something ghostly in all this mess?

I reach for my phone, ready to pull up the video function. I want to have proof that we've caught Amelia doing something she's not supposed to. I almost feel bad for her. Her mother is going to lose her mind.

"Come on," I whisper to Aubrey, and we tiptoe around boxes and crates, big items like full-length mirrors, and a creepy portrait of a man whose eyes follow you around the room. I notice a light at the back of the room and head for it. To my surprise, it's a small open window, almost like an escape hatch.

I peer out. It's a two-story drop to the blacktop, but there's a metal fire escape outside the window. The ladder is wobbling just a little bit as if someone has just climbed down. I also hear footsteps ringing on the pavement. Amelia!

"Let's go," Aubrey says, pushing past me and wriggling out the window.

"Uhhh..." I feel hesitant. I really don't like ladders or heights.

Cody's voice crackles over the radio. "Big Chicken! Mama Hen! What's going on?"

"Amelia just gave us the slip!" I respond. "It's super sketchy! She's on the other side of the stage—heading your way!"

"Makeup can wait," Cody says. "I'm on it."

"*Cody!*" I hear Vee protest on his end. "*Come back!*"

With Aubrey halfway down the ladder and Cody heading Amelia off at the pass, I feel like they have it covered. "I'll come down the stairs and meet you outside," I shout down to Aubrey, happy I don't have to climb down myself. "If you catch her, keep her there. Stall her."

"You got it!" Aubrey grins.

My skin tingles as I hurry out of the props room. This is...*exciting*. Like I'm actually Sadie, solving a crime.

But I'm only a few steps beyond the craft services table when someone grabs my arm. It's Paul. Standing next to him is Morton York. They're both looking at me suspiciously.

"There you are, Hayley!" Paul says. "Where are you off to so fast?"

"Uh..." My mind is blank. I can't think of a single answer. I need to get out of here. Have Aubrey and Cody caught Amelia? What if she got away? Why was she in the props room? "What's up?"

"Schedule change," Paul explains. "Your scene is now, and we're running late." He frowns, glancing at the walkie-talkie in my hand. "What's *that* for?"

Oops. "N-Nothing." I turn the walkie-talkie off. Then I paste on a smile. This is the show's creator, and the last thing I want is to let him down. "Sorry I'm late. I'm ready. No problem."

Austin, the same PA who drove us around on the golf cart, escorts me toward my bedroom set, where I'll be filming a scene where I'm putting together clues. But I feel impatient. I want to be solving the *other* mystery, not my TV one.

Focus, Hayley, I tell myself. Cody and Aubrey surely have this covered. As I pass Video Village, I notice that Mr. York has settled back down in the seat next to Amelia's mother. I give them both a tight smile. Mrs. Hart smirks at me like she's enjoying the fact that I'm messing up again.

Vee intercepts me in the hall to give my makeup a touch-up. "Your buddy sure is acting odd today," she murmurs as she quickly roots through her makeup bag. "Jumped out of my chair like he was a jack-in-the-box!"

"Did you see Amelia on your way in here?" I ask her.

"Hmm...nope. Sorry." She brushes blush on my cheeks and stands back. "There. You look good. Now go, go, go!"

Just because Vee didn't see Amelia doesn't mean anything, I tell myself. But I can't help but wonder what's going on outside. I have a view of the main door, and neither Cody nor Aubrey have come back in. Neither has Amelia, for that matter.

"Come on, Hayley, they're waiting," Austin says, hurrying me down the hall toward my on-set bedroom.

It's the first time I'll be shooting a bedroom scene at Silver Screen Studios, and as I poke my head inside, I'm happy to see that it looks exactly like Sadie's bedroom from the old set. The same gray-and-yellow bedspread. The same posters on the wall. The same cat-shaped piggy bank that Sadie adds to when appreciative citizens pay her a little for solving their cases.

But I don't get any farther into the room. At that very moment, there's a deafening *crack* from above. I see a flash of something solid and black out of the corner of my eye, and suddenly, *whomp:* something huge lands on Sadie's beautiful gray-and-yellow comforter...and shatters into a zillion pieces.

Shards of glass scatter, and I wheel back, afraid I'm going to get cut. It takes me a moment to realize what just fell: a giant lamp from the ceiling. The bulb sparks angrily. Wires twist on the ground like they're alive.

For a few seconds, everyone around me—Austin, Monique the director, Jasper the cameraman, and Vee—stare in stunned silence.

Finally, Monique speaks. "What on *earth*?"

"How could that have fallen?" Austin marvels, staring up.

I look up at the rafters where the light came from too. It's pitch-black. No one's up there. But this doesn't feel like an accident either.

Then I look at the light that's fallen. It's made of thick metal. If it were to hit someone on the head, it would definitely hurt someone, if not knock them out.

And then I realize: Had I been on time, that light would have hit *me*.

CHAPTER ELEVEN

"HAYLEY?" MY MOTHER POKES HER HEAD ABOVE THE TREE house ladder. "Brought you some snacks." Then she looks around at all of us and frowns. "Everyone okay?" She must notice our tense expressions. "Is this about that light falling during shooting today?"

Of course my mother was informed about the light that fell. I mean, her daughter almost got a head injury, and Paul is pretty much required to call her. My mom fled her shop—she works part-time as a florist, when she isn't supervising me—and rushed to the set to offer moral support. She even said we could go home.

But there was no way I was leaving the set altogether. That would mean my scene would be delayed, and the show was already behind schedule. So I pushed my fears down deep and shot the scene. But it wasn't easy. Every second, I was afraid another light was going to fall on my head. I flipped between fearing that Betty was real to worrying that someone was pretending to be Betty...and wanted to hurt me. Who hated me that much?

After my friends were finished with their scenes, I rounded them up, and we came back to the tree house so we could figure out what to do next.

Mom's still staring at us curiously. I realize we haven't answered her question. "We're a little shaken up, yeah," I say. "But it'll be okay." The last thing I want is for my mother to think we're scared. She might pull me off *Sadie Solves It*. And then the show will shut down, and Cody will have to go to Texas, and we'll never see him again.

"Okay," my mother says. She probably senses I'm not saying everything that I feel, but I'm happy she doesn't push it. She leaves a basket of mini bags of chips and cans of fizzy water and soda on the tree house floor. "Yell if you need me, all right?"

When she disappears down the ladder, I slump back on the couch. "Is our show doomed?" Cody moans. "Should I book my ticket back to Texas now?"

"We need to think positive," I say, although I don't really feel positive. "Let's go over what we know. That light fell exactly where I was supposed to be sitting. It feels like someone is sending a message."

"To scare you away?" Aubrey asks.

"Or maybe to get me to stop asking questions," I suggest.

"You really think Amelia would want to hurt you?" Cody asks.

"But it wasn't Amelia, remember? She wasn't anywhere near Stage Five when this happened. We chased her down that fire escape."

"Oh. Right."

Aubrey and Cody exchange a glance I don't quite understand. After the light fell and the dust cleared—literally—I found out that they'd grabbed Amelia as she streaked past them after climbing down from the props room. Aubrey told me that Amelia had stolen something, but she hadn't said exactly what it was.

"We'll let Amelia tell you," Cody had added. "But we're pretty sure it has nothing to do with the ghost."

"Actually, I asked around," Aubrey interrupts my thoughts now. "To cut one of those lights, you have to go to a crawl space up a staircase in a different part of the stage. Totally on the other end from the props room."

"So who was it?" I try to consider everyone in the soundstage. There were tons of people, though. Too many suspects.

"Could it have been an accident?" Cody wonders aloud. "Like, maybe that light had come loose earlier, and for some reason, it chose that moment to fall?"

"*Or* maybe it's a ghost," Aubrey says.

Cody groans.

"Just hear me out!" Aubrey protests. "What if the story about Betty is true? A dancer out for revenge? It'd make sense that she'd go after you, Hayley, as you're the star of the show."

"That makes me feel so much better," I mutter.

Aubrey raises her hands. "Hey, it's why I said we should reach out to her to start with! To get on her side!"

"Aubrey..." Cody covers his eyes. "That's so ridiculous."

"Let's at least do the spirit board," Aubrey pleads. "What if we can contact Betty? Maybe we can convince her to leave us alone."

Cody heaves a big sigh. "Fine. Since you won't shut up about it. But this doesn't mean I believe in it."

"Really?" Aubrey sounds thrilled. "*Yes!*"

She runs to the cabinet and pulls out the board. Then she places it on the coffee table, and we all scoot in and put our fingers on the little plastic planchette.

"Okay." Aubrey rolls her shoulders like she's warming up for a part in a play. "Close your eyes, everyone. I will now call the spirits. *Spirits, please, is there anyone who'd like to speak to us?*"

We wait. Our fingers don't move. Not a centimeter.

"Hello?" I say in a singsong voice. "Sprits?"

We want another minute, but still nothing. I look at Aubrey. "I don't think she's here."

"Yeah," Aubrey says sadly. "Guess not."

But then the planchette jerks. I feel my fingers being pulled in a direction. I open my eyes as the little window in the planchette hovers over the letter *B*.

"B!" Aubrey turns pale. "Like Betty!"

Even Cody looks freaked. Especially when the planchette next moves to the letter *E*. "Guys," Aubrey whispers. "*Told* you she was real."

"It's moving again!" I hiss, letting my fingers drift with the planchette.

But this time, it moves over another *E*. "B-E-E?"

Aubrey sounds confused. Even more confused when the planchette moves to the next letter—a *P*—and then stops.

"B-E-E-P?" Aubrey looks like her head is going to explode. "*Beep?* What does that mean? Betty, are you in a car?"

Cody snorts out a laugh. He pulls his hands off the planchette and covers his mouth to hold in more chuckles. "Got you!" he cries. "I was moving it the whole time!"

"What?" Aubrey looks crushed. "Cody! How could you?"

"I am the spirit Beep!" Cody says in a jokey, spooky voice. *"I am the ghost of junkyard cars!"*

"Ha ha." Aubrey sticks out her tongue. "You really had me going." Then she says, "Be another ghost."

"On the spirit board?" Cody grins. "Sure!"

We put our hands on the board again. This time, we "conjure" a ghost named Spaghetti. She was born in 1654 and owned sixty cats. Then we talk to Moe, who doesn't tell us anything about his past life but informs us that he's positive Aubrey has a crush on someone.

"I do not!" Aubrey cries, eyes shining.

"Moe doesn't lie," Cody insists. "Moe is saying that it's Trevor, one of the extras!"

"No way!" Aubrey sounds like she might throw up. But truth be told, I've seen her flirting with Trevor, just like Moe says.

We put our fingers on the planchette again and again, and Cody sneakily moves it to spell out other ghosts' names and predictions. Does Betty ever show up? Nope.

But we have a lot of fun. And maybe we need a little of fun right now.

One thing's for sure: It's nice not to think about *real* ghosts for a while.

CHAPTER TWELVE

THE NEXT MORNING, MOM PULLS INTO THE SILVER SCREEN Studios lot. She turns to give me a long, careful look.

"Are you sure about this, Hayley?" she asks.

I scrunch my fingers into Salmon's fur. My cat sits on my lap during car rides, otherwise he gets sick. "I don't know what you mean."

"Come on. That light falling from the ceiling. I'm worried about you getting hurt." She bites her lip and stares at the big Silver Studios water tower that looms over us. "You'd think they'd take better care of this place, considering all the shows they shoot here."

"It's totally fine. Just a freak accident." I pick up Salmon and push him into his cat carrier. Salmon wriggles his backside, fighting me all the way. He hates his carrier. I think he thinks he's actually human and doesn't understand why he has to be toted around like luggage. But he also likes to jump out of my arms, so it's the safest thing.

I give Mom a confident smile and slam the door. I can't let that falling light scare me. If someone is pretending to be a ghost, that's exactly what they want to happen.

Actually, it's probably what a *real* ghost wants to happen too.

Whatever, I tell myself. It *isn't* a real ghost. I need to be on Team Cody—ghosts don't exist.

I head into my trailer, set the cat carrier down on the couch, and unzip the front flap. Salmon darts out immediately and runs to his bowl, which one of the PAs has already filled with chopped tuna, his favorite food. (Even though I named him Salmon, he *hates* salmon!)

I notice that the PA has also left my lines for the day

on the couch. I snatch them up, excited to read Sadie's next steps in the mystery. Who could have stolen that book of magic pizza spells? Now, Sadie's turning her attention to Maggie Hornsby, who entered a recipe in an online pizza-making contest. Sadie and her friends have snuck into Candlelight, a fancy restaurant in town. A bunch of townspeople are there too—cranky Mrs. Archer, the librarian who was on duty when the book of spells was stolen, Mr. Grimes, who owns a sandwich shop, and Maggie Hornsby, who's eating with her husband. Sadie's eager to see if Maggie has any magical pizza dust on her fingers.

But as I leaf through the scene, it seems like Maggie has an airtight alibi—she was out of town during the time frame when the book was stolen. She couldn't have done it. Another dead end!

There are more pages in my script, though. I have one more scene to shoot today besides the one in the restaurant. It looks like Sadie is visiting her old friend, a psychic named Madame Curio. *Yes.* I love the woman who plays Madame Curio, a famous actress named Siobhan Cross who hosts dance parties in her trailer after our scenes have wrapped and tells all of us hilarious stories about working with major movie stars. This is going to be great!

In the scene, Madame Curio is going to tell Sadie that the book of spells is still in town somewhere, but that Sadie needs to think outside the box. "The *pizza* box, that is," go Madame Curio's lines. "You see a book of pizza spells, and you think pizza maker. But maybe that's what who stole it *wants* you to think."

Think outside the box. Can that help in this case too? Is someone scaring us for reasons we haven't come up with yet?

But before I can brainstorm, someone yelps out the window. Then I hear a scream. Someone yells, "Fire! Run!"

Fire?

I jump up from the couch and push open my door.

I gasp when I see thick, black smoke pouring from Stage Five. Everyone is running into the alley. Some people have their shirts over their mouths.

I grab Siobhan Cross—aka Madame Curio—as she steps onto the road. "What's going on? And hi, by the way. I've missed you."

"You too." Siobhan Cross looks like she's going to burst into tears. "Oh Hayley, I don't know how it happened. It just suddenly caught fire right in front of me!"

"It's okay, Siobhan." Paul swoops over and pats her shoulder. He's with Mr. York, Monique, and a few of the writers. Everyone looks shaken. "You're not hurt, are you? Is everyone okay?"

"There's really a fire?" I ask, though maybe this is a silly question because of the black smoke. I also hear sirens in the distance.

Paul nods. He has a bleak look on his face. "Electrical fire. A bunch of wires—seemed fine a minute before, but then, *poof*!"

STAGE 5

"It was really strange," Mr. York adds. "I've never seen anything like it."

"Anyway," Paul says, "all the electricity in the stage is down."

"All the electricity?" I cry. This is bad. *Really* bad. One thing a TV show needs to function is electricity. It powers the lights, the cameras, the video screens, the microphone... basically everything.

A fire truck makes a wide turn onto the little alleyway that runs alongside Stage Five. A few firefighters jump out and tramp into the building with hoses, which can't be good. That might ruin our new sets too. Sadie's bedroom. The pizza shops. All because of a stupid electrical fire.

That popped up out of nowhere, it sounds like. Almost like...*a ghost did it.*

CHAPTER THIRTEEN

It doesn't take the firefighters long to put out the blaze in Stage Five. When they march out, they're shrugging their shoulders. "Yep, looks like some sort of faulty wiring," the chief tells Paul. "Any idea when this place was last inspected?"

"I-I was told it was inspected before we moved in." Paul looks panicked. "I don't understand how this sort of thing could have happened."

By the time Paul gathers all of the actors, writers, producers, and crew around in the parking lot outside the building, he has even more bad news. "Looks like the electricians won't be able to get everything up and running for another few days," he reports. "Which actually is warp speed, considering the damage in there."

Everyone starts to murmur. *A few days?* What are we going to do in the meantime?

Amelia's mother raises her hand like an eager student. "What about shooting our scenes on another stage, perhaps?" She gestures to the building next door. "I've noticed Stage Six is empty."

"That's the animal show—you know, the one with trained dogs, monkeys? They're due back here next week. Sorry." Paul shakes his head. "And all the other stages are booked for other shows. Besides, even if there *was* a free stage, we'd have to rebuild all our sets, move the whole operation... It would cost too much."

Cody speaks next. "Maybe we could shoot all the outdoor shots in the next few days? And then go back to all the interior stuff when the electricity is fixed?"

Paul nods. "We can do that. But unfortunately, this episode doesn't have too many outdoor shots. What we really need is to get in those indoor scenes."

"Can some of the indoor scenes move outdoors?" I suggest. "Like Sadie meeting with Madame Curio today. Maybe they could be in, like, a tent in the Woods."

"Good idea, Hayley, though Madame Curio doesn't strike me as the kind of person who goes camping," Paul

says. He squeezes the bridge of his nose. "This is putting us really, *really* behind schedule, and that's not good. The network is being really strict about spending money. They also have a bunch of other shows they're working on that they're excited about, so..." He trails off, not saying the rest.

I glance at my friends in horror. Is he saying what I *think* he's saying? Whenever Paul brings up the network, it makes everyone nervous. After all, the network are the people who pay for *Sadie Solves It* to be on the air. They're the ones who approve all our story ideas, weigh in on casting, and green-light future seasons. They also have the power to cancel a show.

"What do you mean?" Aubrey asks. "Are you saying that the network might shut us down if we can't keep to the schedule?"

Paul sighs heavily. "It's a possibility."

My heart starts to pound. *Canceled.* Everything I've worked for. Everything my friends have worked for. Jobs for all the cast and crew...gone.

"What can we do?" I cry. "There has to be some way to make sure that doesn't happen!"

"We'll shoot the outdoor scenes in the meantime," Paul assures me. He looks around at the whole group, a stern expression on his face. "But when the electricity is working again, no more delays. No more freak-outs." His gaze moves to Amelia, and I see her shrink. "No more trouble. Okay? This is important."

I'm nodding so hard it feels like my head might wobble off my neck. When I look to my right, Cody is biting hard on his lip. He looks scared. Really scared. And I know exactly what he's nervous about.

I reach over, grab his hand, and squeeze it hard. *It'll be okay,* my squeeze says. *I won't let us get canceled.* And I mean that with all my heart.

My friendships depend on it.

CHAPTER FOURTEEN

That night, Mom drops Salmon and me off at Aubrey's house. She lives in Tarzana, a suburb of LA, and her front yard is filled with ride-on toys, stuffed animals, a half-filled kiddie pool, Popsicle wrappers, and a bashed-in piñata in the shape of a *Minecraft* creeper. It looks like some kids had a wild birthday party out here, but actually, this is just a regular Tuesday at Aubrey's place. She has three younger siblings and two older ones, so her family is more chaotic than a tornado.

I ring the doorbell and stand back. Thunderous feet sound from inside, and when the door whips open,

Aubrey's seven-year-old twin sisters, Calla and Carly, start shrieking excitedly. They want to pet my hair, admire my bracelets, and most important, they want to see Salmon, who is pouting inside his cat carrier.

"Okay, okay, great to see you girls too," I wade past them as they pepper me with questions about *Sadie Solves It.* "Will you take care of Salmon while I talk to Aubrey?" I ask them.

"Can we dress Salmon in a tutu?" Carly asks.

"If Salmon's okay with it, sure," I answer.

"What about a superhero costume?" says Calla.

"Go wild." I look around. "Where is Aubrey, anyway?"

"She's in the kitchen," Carly volunteers.

Calla steps closer and says in a whisper, "She's *stress* baking."

Uh-oh. Aubrey loves to bake, but sometimes she goes kind of overboard. And as I walk into her family's kitchen, it looks like a cookie factory has exploded. Not only is the counter covered with flour, sugar, a variety of baking chips, and a large puddle of what smells like vanilla extract, ingredients are all over the floors, the fridge handles, and even on the ceiling. There are also at least five dozen chocolate chip cookies cooling on wire racks in the corner.

Aubrey stands by a large stand mixer. She's wearing a chef's hat and is trying to push a rolling pin over a lopsided glob of dough. There's flour all over her face and hair, and when she turns the mixer on again, ingredients fly everywhere. I duck to avoid flying chunks of oats and brown sugar.

Cody appears from the dining room, where he too has been hiding from the wild mixer tornado. "I tried to stop her, Hayley. I really did."

I walk over to Aubrey as she pushes the cookie mixture around the bowl with a wooden spoon. "I think you've made enough batches, Aud. You can probably stop now."

"But I haven't made any with oats and peanut butter chips," Aubrey insists. More ingredients fly up from the wildly spinning mixer, splattering her cheeks.

"Step away from the mixer," I instruct. "Before someone gets hurt."

Reluctantly, Aubrey turns the mixer's switch off. I lead her to the kitchen table—which is also covered in cookie ingredients—and sit her down in a chair. Cody and I sit next to her. When I breathe in, I have to admit, the freshly baked cookies smell amazing.

"This is going to be okay," I tell Aubrey. "Really."

Aubrey's chin starts to wobble. "How do you know? We still have no idea what's going on, and we have no idea how to stop whatever this is. What if we really are canceled? I don't want Cody to leave! I don't want to split up our friend group! What if I never get another role again as good as Kiki?"

It's hard to see Aubrey so worked up. Sometimes I forget she worries about stuff as much as Cody and I do. And while there's part of me who also wants to melt into a puddle, I know that I need to be the strong one here.

"Cody isn't leaving us," I declare. "*Sadie Solves It* isn't getting canceled. We just have to figure this out. And that means starting at the beginning with our suspects. It's like Madame Curio tells Sadie in the episode—we need to start thinking outside the pizza box."

"Huh?" Cody cocks his head. I've forgotten—he hasn't read that part of the script yet. And we didn't get around to shooting it today.

"It means we need to go through everything again," I explain. "So let's think about why this could be happening. None of this is a coincidence. *Someone* is making stuff fall and things catch fire and lights flicker. We need to figure out why...and who."

"Amelia's off the list," Cody says. "She wasn't anywhere near the light falling, and she wasn't anywhere near the fire starting today."

"But does that mean she actually saw a face in the rafters?" Aubrey argues.

"She *thinks* she saw a face," Cody says. "It could have been a reflection...or a projection. Someone faking a ghost." He shakes his head. "But I don't get why someone would want to scare us."

Aubrey gets a thoughtful look. "It seems that whoever is doing this wants to scare the actors. Think about it—first Amelia is spooked, then you, and then Siobhan. And I know a certain *ghost* who hates actors."

"Betty," I say. "Look, we'll keep her on the list, but I still don't think that's the answer. I think it's a living person. Though you're right about someone trying to scare the actors. Why would someone want to do that?"

"Maybe it's someone who doesn't like actors in general?" Cody suggests. "Like...a failed actor, maybe. Someone who didn't get cast in *Sadie Solves It*?"

"That's interesting," I say, writing it down.

"Or maybe it's someone who *wants* to get cast in *Sadie Solves It,* and they're trying to spook one of us into quitting so they can take our role," Aubrey says.

"Do we remember anyone being really bitter in auditions?" I ask. "Someone who almost got the part but didn't?"

Aubrey thinks a moment. "Not really."

"I don't either," I admit. "But it's a good idea. Someone could be mad at an actor. One of *us*." I look around at the group, feeing my stomach clench. "Do either of you have any enemies?"

"*Me?*" Aubrey cries. "No way." But then she pauses. "Except... There was that girl who I tripped in my big soccer tournament. She was on the other team, and making this huge play, and I swear it was an accident, but..."

"And there was that kid in the vintage shop who was eyeing those classic Nikes, but *I* got to them first. He was so mad." Cody looks worried. "But would he really want to scare me out of my role?"

"What about you, Hayley?" Aubrey asks.

I think for a moment. The only person I bicker with, really, is Amelia—and we've already ruled her out. But what if it's someone I'm not even thinking of? Maybe someone who doesn't like that I bring Salmon to the set. Someone who's jealous that I got the part as Sadie.

Someone who's mad at me for something I don't even know I did.

Maybe it could be anyone.

I stand, and my friends look at me. "Have you figured something out?" Cody asks excitedly.

"Yeah." I walk over to one of the cooling racks and start loading up a plate. "It's definitely, *definitely* time for cookies."

CHAPTER FIFTEEN

Finally, production is up again. There's a buzz of excitement in the air as we head back into Stage Five, but it's laced with tension. Everyone, from the actors to the writers to Vee in hair and makeup, is early for their call times. No one wants to put us behind schedule and get *Sadie Solves It* canceled.

But *someone* is making all this stuff happens. And I need to find out who.

Vee swipes blush on my cheekbones as I look over my lines. Siobhan—Madame Curio—isn't available today, so we're shooting different scenes instead and saving her scene for later. In today's scene, Sadie, Pepper, and her other friends have a run-in with the cranky librarian, Mrs. Archer, in the town square. At first, Sadie pleasantly comments about how it's too bad the security footage from the night the pizza book was stolen is damaged—it would be so helpful in solving the mystery. To Sadie's surprise, Mrs. Archer acts sketchy. She doesn't answer Sadie's question, and then she runs.

Security footage. Just reading it gives me an idea.

I have a few minutes before my first scene is going to film, so I tell Vee I'll be right back. I head over to Cody's trailer. When I push the door open, I notice that he's sitting on the couch, FaceTiming with Chris, one of his moms.

"It's going fine, I promise," Cody says to the screen. He sounds upset.

"But are you sure things are safe after the fire?" Chris says. "And Hayley's mom called and said a light nearly fell on her head!"

I lick my lips. My mom is talking about the show with Cody's moms? What if she convinces them to pull Cody from *Sadie Solves It*?

"I mean it, everything's going fine here. *Great,* in fact. I don't want you to worry—or stop our plans to move. Did you get those apartment listings I sent? Some of them look big enough for all of us."

Chris says she has to go, and Cody clicks off and shuts his eyes. Then he notices me at the door and grimaces. "How much did you hear?"

"Only that your mom seems as worried as mine," I say, walking into the room. "This better not stand in the way of you moving here permanently."

There's a knock on the door, and it's Aubrey. "Um, Paul is looking for you, Hayley," she says. "Your scene is soon."

"I know. I just want to share something quickly." I square my shoulders. "I have an idea about how we might get some clues."

"Clues for what?" comes another voice. And then I realize—Amelia is standing behind Aubrey, that typical nosy look on her face. *Ugh.* I blew it.

"Clues for *what*?" Amelia asks again. "What are you guys talking about?"

Bad, *bad* move. Aubrey isn't going to take no for an answer. Even worse, if we don't tell her what we're up to, she might spread untrue gossip.

I sigh. "We're trying to figure out this ghost thing. We don't think it's a real ghost. We think it's someone pretending to be a ghost to scare us away."

Amelia's eyes widen. "Who would do that?"

"We don't know." I turn to my friends. "But I was thinking—we should ask the guys at the security gate if they've seen anyone unfamiliar lurking around Silver Screen Studios. Like, say it *is* someone angry with us, someone one of us knows from somewhere else—maybe they could help identify the person."

"Good thought," Cody says.

"I want to help," Amelia pipes up.

"No way," I tell her. "This was just for us three. We don't want to get you in trouble."

Amelia crosses her arms. "Guess it doesn't matter that I happen to be buddy-buddy with Timothy, then."

Aubrey frowns. "Who's Timothy?"

"Oh, you know," Amelia says airily. "Only the head of gate security. He and I are both really into astrology. He's an Aquarius too! We bonded. Now we're besties."

"And you think Timothy will give us information?" Cody sounds like he really, *really* hates that he has to ask this question.

"He'll give *me* information," Amelia corrects. "Don't know about the rest of you." He eyes Aubrey in particular. "He really doesn't trust an Aries."

Salmon saunters into the room and slinks around our legs. Amelia jerks away from him, as usual. I breathe out a sigh. There's really no way around this, is there? "Fine, Amelia. But you say a word about this to anyone, and you'll regret it."

"*Yes!*" Amelia whoops.

Looks like Sadie's little sister is joining the crew.

After everyone shoots their morning scenes, we have a break for lunch. We huddle outside Stage Five and head over to the studio's head security gate. Paul walks out of the writer's offices just then and notices all four of us—including Amelia—walking together. He smiles. "Nice to see you all getting along."

If only he knew the truth.

"So you really think it's someone who's mad at one of us?" Amelia chirps after Paul passes. "I mean, *I'm* the one who saw the ghost the most. But who could be mad at me? My mom says I'm totally loveable!"

Aubrey nudges me in the ribs. Kind of doubtful that *everyone* loves Amelia.

True to his word, when the head guard in the little hut at the drive-on gate looks up and sees Amelia, he beams. "My fellow Aquarius!" he cries. "How are you?"

"Good, Timothy," Amelia says, giving the rest of us a knowing look. "How are *you*?"

She leans on his little window, and for the next few minutes, the two of them talk horoscopes, rising signs, and Mercury being in retrograde. I've never been so impatient in my life. Finally, I blurt, "Amelia, can you ask Timothy our question, please?"

"Oh. Right." Amelia straightens.

But when she asks Timothy if anyone suspicious or unfamiliar has come on the lot lately, he shakes his head.

"We haven't allowed anyone new on the set since you guys arrived. A top secret movie is shooting over on Stage Seventeen. Huge stars. The kind that are always in the gossip magazines. They put it into their contract not to allow *any* visitors." He points at Amelia. "We even had to convince them to let your mom on the set!"

"Really?" Amelia looks dazzled. "Who are the movie stars?"

"Afraid I can't tell. But anyway, no one we don't know has come through these gates. We've made *extra* sure."

We thank Timothy and turn back toward Stage Five. A golf cart buzzes by. A few people wearing staff T-shirts for *Chat with Matt,* a popular talk show that also shoots at Silver Screen Studios, stroll past. I even see Mr. York and Mike, the guy who builds our sets, strolling from the direction of the cafeteria. They seem deep in discussion. Mr. York wears a fancy suit. Mike's got on jeans and a dingy T-shirt. They make a strange pair.

"What a shame," Aubrey sighs. "I thought for sure

Timothy would give us some kind of clue. It's hard to believe *no one* unfamiliar has come onto the set!"

"Actually, we did get a clue," I say, stopping short. Something has just come to me. "A *big* one."

CHAPTER SIXTEEN

Amelia stares at me like I've sprouted a green unicorn horn on my head. "What are you talking about? What clue did Timothy give us?"

I spin around and point at the security hut behind us. At that very moment, a car pulls up. Timothy steps out of his hut and checks the driver's ID. Then he nods, waving the man inside. I recognize the guy from the cafeteria. He's definitely Silver Screen Studios staff.

"Whoever is doing this ghost stuff?" I say. "It's got to be a regular. Someone who has a Silver Screen Studios ID."

Amelia wrinkles her nose. "Someone we know? Who? And why?"

I almost tell Amelia that for a little while, we thought *she* would...for attention. "We'll have to figure that out," I admit.

"But surely it's not anyone who was with us last season!" Cody says. "Nothing like this happened at our old studio. It only started when we got here."

"True," I say. And as far as I can tell, none of the old crew seems unhappy. Everyone is just as excited to work on *Sadie Solves It* as they've ever been. "Maybe we should focus on the new people for now."

"Well, *that's* going to be easy." Amelia rolls her eyes. "That's, like, fifty percent of the people on the show. Good job narrowing it down, Hayley."

"Do you want to be part of this investigation or not?" I snap at her. Then I think of something else. "And by the way. Why did you steal something from the props room? And why in the world did you sneak down the ladder?"

Amelia stops. She glances toward Aubrey and Cody. "I…um… it doesn't matter."

I put my hands on my hips. "What are you keeping from me?"

"Just tell her, Amelia," Aubrey mumbles.

Amelia slaps her arms to her sides and lowers her head guiltily. Then, another golf cart whizzes past. It's Monique, our director. "Hey, crew!" she calls at us. The moment has broken. Amelia's saved.

"Hey!" Amelia says, running after her without answering.

I look at my friends. "What's she hiding?"

Aubrey shrugs. "We told her we'd let her tell you herself. It's…complicated."

I have no idea what she means, but I have no time to dwell on it. We're at the door to Stage Five, and it's time to go in.

As usual, PAs are rushing around, lighting guys are stringing cords and wires, and a couple of the writers are sitting on directors' chairs in Video Village. I look around, taking stock just like Sadie would. Some of these people I know from before, but not *all* of them. Like the new woman, Hazel, who operates the boom arm—that's the long stick attached to the microphone, which dangles over actors' heads as they say their lines. If the boom operator does her job correctly, you'll *never* see the microphone in the shot—it's just out of frame.

I don't know Hazel very well. And she's standing in the corner, glancing shiftily at something on her phone. Could *she* be the ghost?

Or there's Will, one of the new writers. I've noticed him before, and he always keeps to himself. Even now, he's quietly munching on a little cup of M&M's from craft services, not talking with the others. Maybe he feels like he doesn't fit in? But would that make you want to scare the pants off everyone on the set?

I notice that Aubrey, Cody, and even Amelia are peering around at people they don't know too, probably thinking the same things. It doesn't give me the greatest feeling. I don't like assuming that the people around me, people working hard to make the show, could be bad. I'd rather think that we're all a big, happy team.

"You guys okay?"

Paul's voice startles me. He must have snuck over while we were busy searching for clues. All of us shuffle and mutter that we're fine, but Paul snorts. "Uh, no you're not. Come with me."

He leads us into his office, which is in a back corner of the soundstage, though on the complete opposite side of where Amelia ran up the secret staircase. We file through the door, and then he shuts it and sits down at his desk. "Okay. Why do you all look like you're keeping a massive secret?"

Everyone exchanges a glance. Then Amelia blurts, "Hayley thinks the ghost is someone working on the set!"

"Amelia!" I whine.

"Sorry." Amelia shrugs. "I thought he should know."

"It's not just Hayley," Aubrey says quickly. "It's Cody and me too. It kind of makes sense. Security's been tight at Silver Screen Studios—we checked. And this has only happened since we've gotten to Hollywood. We're just worried someone is trying to shut down the show. We care about *Sadie Solves It.* We don't want anything bad to happen."

Paul rubs his eyes. "I was afraid you guys were going down that path. All the ghost rumors, plus the fact that we're working on a mystery show...but listen. These are old buildings. A lot of stuff hasn't been properly updated. I know it's

a legendary studio, but I've reached out to the studio head to say that Stage Five is an unacceptable workplace. We need some repairs. *That's* what I think is happening. Lights are falling because the cords holding them up are ancient and frayed. Lights flicker all the time in old buildings like these. And fires are starting not because of a ghost but because the last time the electricity was updated was thirty years ago! The electrician told me so after the fire."

"Really?" Cody asks, tilting his head. "That's not good."

"But what about the face Amelia saw in the rafters?" Aubrey asks. "And the *whoosh* we all felt? How can an old building do that?"

"As for the whoosh, it was probably just an air current. And as for the face you saw..." He glances at Amelia and trails off.

Amelia crosses her arms. "You're going to say I'm just going to be dramatic, aren't you? Spoken like a true Leo."

Paul holds up his palms. "I love your energy, guys.

I love that you're becoming detectives just like your characters. But let the higher-ups handle this stuff, okay? I'm waiting on a call from the studio head, and I have a feeling everything will go smoothly from there. There's no ghost. No one *pretending* to be a ghost." He winks. "I promise."

"No more ghost," we all mutter.

I know we should be relieved, but I don't feel that way at all. It doesn't take me long to figure out why.

I don't believe him. Not the slightest bit.

CHAPTER SEVENTEEN

Soon after speaking with Paul, all of us are scheduled for wardrobe, or for school time with our tutor, or, in Amelia's case, for "mom and daughter time" with Mrs. Hart. I'm standing in wardrobe as Romy, our beloved costume designer, fits me in a vintage plaid blazer and some ripped jeans.

"I love how the green in the jacket picks up the flecks in her eyes," says Vee, who's leaning against the wardrobe door. I'm going to her next for hair and makeup. "By the way, Hayley, you're not still worried about the lights, are you? I'd think that'd be all fixed now that the electricity's been updated."

I run my tongue over my teeth. "All good." As much as I want to share my theory with Romy and Vee, I'm afraid they'll be on Paul's side. And also, Romy's new assistant, Kelsey, is here too. She started only after we moved to Silver Screen Studios—so technically, as a newbie, she's on the suspect list.

But at the same time, I don't want to suspect Kelsey. She spent the first fifteen minutes of my fitting cooing over Salmon and showing me pictures of her French bulldog, Baxter. How could someone who regularly dresses her dog in a tuxedo be a bad person?

After today's outfit is chosen, Austin the PA hands me some of the afternoon's scenes. I rip through them, eager to learn how this mystery ends. We've investigated everyone in the pizza game in town, but we've run into dead ends every time.

In the final scenes, Sadie returns to all the clues: the

footprints leading out of the library, which definitely seem like the types of clogs that a chef might wear. How a ripped page of the book was found at Giovanni's pizzeria, but Giovanni and his entire staff had an alibi for the evening the book went missing—and so did everyone from Sal's, as Sadie thought that maybe the rival pizzeria might have planted the page at Giovanni's to throw the detectives off the trail. Sadie thinks again about Madame Curio's wisdom about thinking beyond the pizza box. And then she considers Mrs. Archer, the cranky librarian who wouldn't answer her questions about the damaged security footage. Could she be hiding something? Could *she* have damaged the footage...to protect someone?

And that's how she solves it.

Sadie remembers when she and her friends went to Candlelight, the fancy restaurant where they questioned Maggie Hornsby. Mrs. Archer had been there too, having dinner with Mr. Grimes, who owns a struggling sandwich shop near Giovanni's. And then it hit Sadie: She'd also seen

Mr. Grimes riding his bike across the square the other day, and he'd been wearing chef's clogs, just like the footprints in the library!

Suddenly, it all made sense. Maybe Mr. Grimes stole the book of spells simply so that neither Sal nor Giovanni could get their hands on it—because if they would, they'd become even *more* popular, taking away even more business from the sandwich shop. It wasn't that he was going to make delicious pizza with the magic recipes. He just didn't want anyone else to!

I tear through my script, excited to see that Sadie, Pepper, and her friends tear across town to question Mr. Grimes. But he gives them the slip at the last minute. They go on a wild-goose chase to track him down, certain he's guilty.

But I won't get to see the final scene, where everything wraps up, until tomorrow. It's so frustrating! Sometimes there's a twist in the final scene. Sometimes, Sadie *thinks* she's solved it, but there's just one more curveball. Which she solves, of course, but always in the final moments.

There's a knock on my trailer door. Austin pokes his head in. "Paul was tied up. He asked me to get you for your scene, Hayley."

"Oh." With a final pat on Salmon's head, I hop off the couch. "Great."

Austin leads me into Stage Five. Halfway up the ramp, he stops and stares at a huge wire lying across the doorway. "*That* wasn't here when I left," he says, kicking it out of the way. Then he looks around. "How did that even get here? That could have really tripped someone up."

The back of my neck prickles. Is this more work of the "ghost"? Moving wires around to cause an injury?

I join my friends and Amelia on the set. We're filming the scene where everyone brainstorms ideas and suddenly remembers Mrs. Archer and Mr. Grimes. I should be excited, but I'm still thinking about the wire in the doorway.

"What's wrong?" Aubrey asks, noticing my expression.

"Nothing," I murmur, though I step closer to her,

Cody, and Amelia. "I think we need to keep our eyes and ears open. That ghost—he or she is still around."

Amelia nods bravely. So do Cody and Aubrey. It's good to have such a dedicated team.

Vee rushes out for makeup touch-ups, and Peter, the hairstylist, fluffs our hair. Jasper is getting the camera in exactly the right place, and I even see Mike, the guy we met on the first day, drift past. The new boom operator, Hazel, is getting her boom stick ready. I look at her closely. She's wearing a button bearing a picture of a gap-toothed little kid.

"Who is that?" I ask her.

Hazel looks up and smiles. "My grandson, Howie!" She touches the button. "He lives far away, but I keep begging his mom to bring him out here so he can visit the set!"

"That's so sweet," I murmur. But in my mind: *Hazel wouldn't sabotage Sadie Solves It if she wants to show it to her grandson!*

At that very moment, someone rushes up to us from

behind, holding a bunch of papers. It's Will, the new writer. "Hey, guys. Um, I have some teeny-tiny line changes. Nothing big, just a few tweaks Paul wanted me to make on this scene."

"*You* wrote this scene?" I ask. "Where they realize it's Mrs. Archer and Mr. Grimes?"

"Yeah." Will ducks his head bashfully. "I hope you like it."

"I love it!" I say. "It's really good!"

Will looks overjoyed. "This is the very first episode I've gotten to write. Every day, I wake up and can't believe I'm an actual writer now and not just someone's assistant." His cheeks go red. "Sorry. TMI! Anyway, here are the scripts."

He passes them to us hurriedly and scuttles away. But again, my mind is churning. *Will wouldn't want the show to shut down. He'd lose his first-ever writing job.*

"Places," Paul calls out from behind the camera. "Hayley? Amelia? Cody and Aubrey? We good?"

"Uh huh," I say, hurrying to my mark.

But I'm distracted. I know Will and Hazel are just two people, but I want to believe that everyone on this set is nice and wants to be here. And maybe they *are*. Is it possible Paul's right? Maybe I *am* seeing things? Maybe all these strange things are just because we're in a cranky old building...and nothing more?

"And...action!" Monique the director calls.

The camera starts rolling. I hear Aubrey say her first line, and then Cody say his first line, and then Amelia hides under a blanket and says she's scared. Then, everyone looks to me, because my line is next.

But suddenly, my line has gone out of my head. My vision is focused on something fluttering along the ceiling. Something...*see-through*. White. With...is that long, flowing *hair?*

Oh no. It's *her*. Again. But at the moment, I seem to be the only one who sees the ghost.

"*Hayley!*" Monique whispers. And then, frustrated. "Cut!"

The bell rings, indicating that we've stopped rolling. Everyone's staring at me, definitely wondering why I've messed up. But I can't stop staring at that filmy, fluttering projection on the ceiling.

A ghost, maybe. Or a *person* pretending to be a ghost.

Whatever it is, I'm going to find out. This ends now.

CHAPTER EIGHTEEN

I TEAR OFF THE SET. BEHIND ME, PAUL IS SCREAMING.

"Hayley!" he cries. "Hayley, what are you doing!"

"I just need to check on something!" I yell. "Hang on!"

"You can't run out in the middle of the scene!" His voice tightens. "This is costing us money!"

I want to tell him that this might *save* us money. But there's no time. In seconds, someone else might look up and see the ghostly image on the ceiling. Then the screams will start. I need to stop whatever this is before that happens. *Someone* is behind this. And I'm going to find out who.

I burst out of the maze of sets to a more open part of the soundstage, which gives me a better sense of where the ghost is on the ceiling and where the reflection could be coming from. Suddenly, a crash sounds from a far corner. A props guy named Steve nearly backs into me, his face pale.

"Th-those crates just fell all on their own," he stammers, pointing at a few splintered boxes several feet from where he's standing. "They could've crushed me!"

"Oh my," I whisper. But they didn't fall on their own. I know it. I give him a sympathetic look and then push past him, toward the falling boxes.

I can hear Paul and others calling my name behind me: "Hayley! Hayley, what are you *doing*?"

But I run toward the falling boxes anyway. I'm going to figure this out.

The crates are stacked high. Scraps of wood from the ones that fell are everywhere. I wheel around, checking out the ghostly reflection still on the ceiling. And then I turn back to a point on the ground, just behind the boxes.

Light is shining out, almost like someone is...yes! There's a projector. Someone is *beaming* the ghost's image onto the soundstage!

But as soon as I take another step, a crate crashes from the top of the pile. I yelp and jump back just before the crate smashes to the floor. It would have knocked me out had it hit me in the head.

"Hayley!" Now it's Amelia. She and everyone else are standing on the other side of the smashed crates, staring at me in horror. "It's dangerous back there! Crates are falling everywhere!"

"It's the ghost," someone else pipes up. "It's got to be!"

"So this place *is* haunted?" another voice cries. "I'm outta here!"

"Hayley," Paul interjects. "Please. You have to stop. You're jeopardizing the show—for real. Every minute we waste with this is costing us money—and you know we're on thin ice."

I nod. I know that. But I have to do this.

I turn from them, facing the huge wall of crates and the light from the projector. Someone's back there. I can see a shadow moving. Whoever it is, he or she knows I'm here—Amelia and Paul and everyone else have blown my cover. I have only seconds before they escape.

Another box smashes to my left. I duck away from it, trying not to feel afraid. I zigzag past the wall of crates until I'm at the very back. There's a thin corridor behind the crates, only big enough for a person to fit through. It's dark in there, but I can just make out a shadow slipping away. I also see a projector screen, definitely the one that has been beaming the ghostly image onto the wall. I also notice a few strong, heavy ropes hanging from the wall of crates, stretching all the way to the top. Perhaps this is how the person was making the crates fall. Maybe they'd rigged some sort of system to push them off from the ground, making it look like they were falling all on their own, the work of a ghost.

The figure is getting away. I hurry down the narrow corridor. "Wait!" I cry out, twisting the sapphire ring

around my finger for extra courage. "I see you! Stop! It's over, okay?"

The figure keeps moving. A door opens, and light from another room floods in. The person slips through to their escape, but not before I catch up to him and spin him around.

When I see who it is, I rear back. "Y-You?" I whisper.

It's Mike. The guy who told us about the ghost in the first place.

CHAPTER NINETEEN

Mike is dressed from head to toe in all black. He stares at me angrily...and guiltily.

"You?" I cry. "*You're* the one who's been doing this?"

"Please," Mike begs. "This isn't what it looks like. I haven't hurt anyone. I'm doing someone a favor, that's all."

"A favor?" I'm confused. "What do you mean? *Who?*"

He looks away. "I can't tell. Just go away, okay? I'll stop. I promise. Just go back to what you were doing."

I grab his arm. "You have to tell me. Everyone's just behind the crates. In seconds, I'm going to call out that you've done it. But if someone put you up to this, you have to tell me who it is."

Mike shakes his head stubbornly. "I can't, Hayley. I'm sorry."

Footsteps sound from the other end of the corridor. A flashlight snaps on, and its bright light makes me squint. A few figures press forward, and I hear a familiar voice boom, "I can't believe someone would do such a thing. I've said all along this ghost is a hoax. This man should be punished."

It's Mr. York, the big-time producer. Paul, Amelia, Aubrey, and Cody are following him, but he's leading the way. It's surprising. I hadn't realized Mr. York was on set today. And how had he gotten here so fast? Why is he at the front of this group? Is this because he knew about Betty from his old show? Only, that doesn't quite make sense either.

Something isn't sitting right. I stare from Mr. York to Mike, then back again. How did Mr. York even know

I was searching for the ghost? I hadn't *said* that's what I was doing. And sure, Mike had confessed just now, but we hadn't been talking loudly enough for anyone else to hear.

"Wait a minute." I look at Mike. "Is *Mr. York* the one who put you up to this?" I point a shaky hand at Mr. York. "Is he making you pretend to be a ghost?"

Mr. York reels back. "Ex*cuse* me?" He puts his hands on his hips. "That's a serious accusation, Hayley. I think you should apologize."

But I can tell by the look on Mike's face that I'm right.

"Oh my goodness," I whisper. I think about the episode we're almost done shooting. About how it was all about who was friends with whom and who owed someone else a favor. I think about how, in one of the scenes, Sadie spotted Mrs. Archer, the librarian, and Mr. Grimes having dinner at Candlelight. One of her lines was that she didn't even realize the two knew each other.

And then I remember just an hour ago—seeing Mike and Mr. York walking back from lunch. I'd thought about what a strange pair they'd made. They didn't seem like they'd be friends. It's exactly the same.

But maybe they aren't friends. Maybe they were talking about ghosts.

I think about all of the ghostly occurrences. Mike hadn't been here for all of them—we'd already checked. But Mr. York had. He was here at every single one, and we'd completely overlooked him because he's such an important person. We totally missed it.

"It was you," I say quietly to Mr. York. "Wasn't it?"

"Hayley." Paul sounds worried. "Maybe you should take a step back."

"She absolutely should," Mr. York barks. He looks at me hard. "You'd better watch what you say, Hayley, or you'll have no future in Hollywood."

"It never made sense why you wanted to work on our show after yours was canceled here," I go on. I'm not backing down that easily. "I never quite bought that you were looking for new stars either—sorry, Amelia."

Mr. York looks furious. "So now you're accusing me of lying?"

I turn back to Mike. "Am I wrong?"

Mike bites hard on his lip. Mr. York lets out a grunt. "*Say* something! Tell her that I had nothing to do with this... *ghost* nonsense!"

Mike glances at him guiltily. "Morton." His voice is low. "I'm not going to lie. Not anymore."

A gasp rises in the crowd. Now everyone turns to Mr. York, who's gone pale. He shakes his head with force and

mutters a few syllables, but it's no use. Finally, he slaps his arms to his sides.

"I didn't think we'd have to take things this far!" he shouts. "I thought you'd be scared off days ago! And then, with the fire—I thought that would do it! But no! You people just kept going! Especially *you*!" He points a finger at me.

Paul's mouth drops open. Amelia looks like she's going to faint. But my friends are standing strong. "Why?" Aubrey asks. "Why did you do it?"

"Why do you think?" Mr. York looks totally unhinged now. His hair is mussed. His eyes are wild, and he no longer looks like a polished Hollywood bigwig. "It's humiliating to have a show canceled! I feel like a total failure! I thought if you left, maybe I'd get my set back! I thought maybe the network would give my show another chance. I put my heart and soul into *Motor Clowns.* It's genius! And if the studio just saw a *few more episodes...*"

I almost burst out laughing. *Motor Clowns?* Is he serious?

"So you faked a ghost?" Cody says, his voice deadpan. "And tried to scare us away?"

"You didn't just fake a ghost." Paul sounds angry now. "You set things on fire. You dropped things from the ceiling. You could have *hurt* someone, Morton."

Mr. York's eyes blaze. "You don't understand. *No one* understands." And then, arms flapping, he storms away.

Paul glances at Austin. "Catch him before he leaves."

"On it," Austin says. "Already called security."

Paul turns back to me, staring at me for a few bewildered moments. "I have to hand it to you, Hayley. You solved this when no one else could."

"Please," I say. "Aubrey and Cody were huge helps. Amelia too." Amelia looks pleased. "And also, this is what's going to happen in the episode too, right? It isn't only Mr. Grimes who's guilty. Sure, he stole the book, but he's just a worker at the sub shop. But Mr. Archer, Mrs. Archer's husband, owns the sandwich shop franchise. He's the one who really put Mr. Grimes up to it."

Will widens his eyes. "Actually, we hadn't quite settled on the end scene yet. But Hayley, that's *perfect*!"

Paul grins at me. "Art imitating life!" He nudges my side. "We might just need you in the writers' room, Hayley!"

"Oh, I'm happy just playing Sadie," I tell him.

And maybe, just maybe, solving mysteries too.

CHAPTER TWENTY

"So I'll take one cookies and cream, a mint chip, a birthday cake, and..." I turn to Amelia, who's standing behind me with an anxious look on her face. "...what flavor did you want again?"

"A coconut gelato, but only if it's organic coconut, and only if it has absolutely no artificial colors," Amelia states knowingly. "I'm highly sensitive to artificial coloring. I'm sure it's an Aquarius thing."

The woman working the Betsy's Homemade Ice Cream truck says in a bored voice that the coconut gelato has no artificial colors. Then she gets to work scooping our cones. I turn around just as a burly moving man clomps down the U-Haul ramp with another giant box in his arms. Like many of the others, this one is labeled "Record Albums."

"Wow," I mutter to Cody, who's also standing on the curb with me, Aubrey, and Amelia. "How many boxes of records does your mom have?"

"Probably a million more." Cody sighs. "I think that's the real reason she didn't want to make the move. She didn't want to pack all her things."

But despite Cody's fake-weary attitude, his cheeks are pink with glee. Today is moving day for Cody's family—for real. It all happened really fast—once we found out that *Sadie Solves It* was no longer in danger of being canceled, Cody's mom went hunting for a place big enough to fit two adults and two kids. We thought the process would take forever, but she got lucky and found a great apartment really fast.

Extra bonus: Apparently the ice cream truck parks here every day. Extra extra bonus: It's not far from my house, meaning Cody can bike to the tree house and we can have secret meetings whenever we want. *Yes!*

We receive our cones, and I pay the woman behind the counter. Then we sit on the curb and watch the boxes stream from the van. I'm so relaxed and happy, I don't even mind that Amelia is with us. If you overlook her annoying pushiness and the fact that she mentions being an Aquarius every five seconds, she isn't so bad.

"So did everyone hear the latest about Mr. York?" Aubrey asks as she licks the bottom of the cone to keep the ice cream from dripping. "He's been banned from Silver Screen Studios for life. Apparently, he was pretending to be a ghost on a few other sets too, including the animal show right next to us on Stage Six. He was trying to get all of them to shut down just like he was doing to us, all in hopes of *Motor Clowns* coming back."

"No way!" Cody's eyes boggle, and then he shakes his head. "I still can't believe *he* was the ghost."

"Seriously." Amelia raises her chin in defiance. "*I* can't believe I was tricked into thinking he was eyeing me up to be the next big star."

"Looks like you're stuck on *Sadie Solves It* for a little while longer. I didn't realize you were so eager to get off the show in the first place." I'm surprised at how defensive I sound.

Amelia looks up in surprise. "I never said I wanted to get off *Sadie Solves It.* I love being on the show."

I frown. "You do? For real? Even though you're not the star?"

"Yeah, in fact..." Amelia trails off. She clamps her mouth shut like there's more that she wants to say, but she doesn't want to say it.

Aubrey and Cody exchange a look. "I'm just going to throw my napkin away," Aubrey then says loudly, rising from the curb.

"Me too," Cody says, hurrying after her.

I watch them as they tromp off to a trash can. Amelia bites loudly into her cone. Once she's done chewing, she says, "I can't believe they didn't tell you."

"Tell me what?" I ask.

"About what I stole from the props room. I mean, I asked them to let me tell you, but I figured they'd spill my secret anyway. You're all so close. I figured you were laughing at me behind my back, or whatever."

"Aubrey and Cody aren't like that," I say. "They're true to their word. When they make a promise, they keep it."

"Oh." Amelia pulls her knees to her chest. "Huh. I didn't know that."

She keeps eating her cone. But I haven't forgotten that Amelia wanted to tell me something. Maybe about what she swiped something from the props room. "I won't laugh," I say. "I promise."

Amelia takes a big breath. "I took Sadie's old necklace," she mumbles. "From season one? The one she was always wearing but kept getting tangled? I wanted to wear it, or whatever. In private." She ducks her head. "Told you it was dumb."

"You wanted to wear Sadie's old necklace?" In the show, Sadie wore a sapphire necklace the first season, and though it was really pretty, it kept getting caught on things mid-scene. That's why we swapped it out for the sapphire ring.

"You just looked so cool with it on." Amelia still won't look at me. "I wanted to see what it felt like to wear it. To *be* that. Be like Sadie." Her cheeks go red. "Like you."

I can feel ice cream dripping onto my hand, but I don't move to wipe it off. I had no idea Amelia admired Sadie—or *me*.

I feel touched.

"I'll give it back," Amelia goes on. "It was dumb. And if anyone should get it, it should be you."

"I don't want it back," I say quickly. "You should have it."

Amelia looks at me, a light coming on in her eyes. "Really?"

I nod. "Totally." And then I add, "You know, it was fun solving the mystery with you. In the show—*and* in real life."

Amelia looks dazzled. "It *was,* wasn't it?"

"Well, you might have more mysteries to solve," says a voice above us. "Don't hang up your detective hats just yet."

I look up. Paul is standing on the street, grinning down at Amelia and me. Aubrey and Cody have wandered back over too. "What are you doing here?" I ask him.

"Had to make sure one of my stars is moving in okay," Paul explains. He turns to Cody's moms. "Everything fine?"

"Peachy." Jada wags a finger at him. "But you had us

scared. Our Cody was losing his mind when he thought the show was going to be canceled!"

"That's no longer a worry," Paul assures her. "Thanks to your son. And a few others." He gives me a wink.

"What did you mean when you said we might have other mysteries?" I ask him. "Has something else happened?" *Please no more ghosts,* I think. I've had enough of things falling from the sky and creepy whooshes of air.

"Nothing like that," Paul says. "And let's hope nothing else *does* happen—certainly nothing that'll shut us down. But we *are* in Hollywood, Hayley. It's a magical place that's full of history, but there's a lot of suspicious stuff that goes on. Maybe you'll be the show's eyes and ears? You did such a good job last time."

I blush. "Well," I admit, "I *do* play a detective on TV. So it's not such a huge jump to be one in real life. Hayley's Detective Agency is open for business!"

Everyone laughs. The movers slam the U-Haul's back door shut, signifying that Cody's family is all moved in.

Everyone goes to give Cody a big hug, but I take a moment to peer out at the Silver Screen Studios water tower in the distance, peeking up over the buildings. I get a shiver of pride every time I see it, and this time is no different. Except the shiver is for anticipation too. Excitement...maybe mixed with a little bit of fear.

What other mysteries are lurking behind those walls? And will we be able to solve them?

ABOUT THE AUTHOR

Hayley LeBlanc is a thirteen-year-old actress, artist, and social media star with more than 5.3 million followers across Instagram and YouTube. Hayley performed in the lead role of Harmony in the two hit Brat TV series *Chicken Girls* and *Mani*. Hayley lives in Los Angeles, where in her spare time she likes to hang out with friends, listen to music, read books, and watch horror and mystery films and TV shows.

DON'T MISS THE NEXT BOOKS IN

THE HAYLEY MYSTERIES SERIES:

THE HAYLEY MYSTERIES
THE SECRET ON SET
HAYLEY LEBLANC